Mighty Mighty MONSTERS

Homesick Witch

Raintree is an imprint of Capstone Global Library Limited, a
company incorporated in England and Wales having its registered
offi ce at 7 Pilgrim Street, London, EC4V 6LB – Registered company
number: 6695582

www.raintree.co.uk
myorders@raintree.co.uk

Text © Capstone Global Library Limited 2015

Printed and bound in China

ISBN 978 1 4062 7991 7
18 17 16 15 14
10 9 8 7 6 5 4 3 2 1

British Library Cataloguing in Publication Data
A full catalogue record for this book is available from the British
Library.

All the internet addresses (URLs) given in this book were valid at
the time of going to press. However, due to the dynamic nature
of the internet, some addresses may have changed, or sites may
have changed or ceased to exist since publication. While the author
and publisher regret any inconvenience this may cause readers, no
responsibility for any such changes can be accepted by either the
author or the publisher.

Mighty Mighty MONSTERS

Homesick Witch

created by
Sean O'Reilly

illustrated by
Arcana Studio

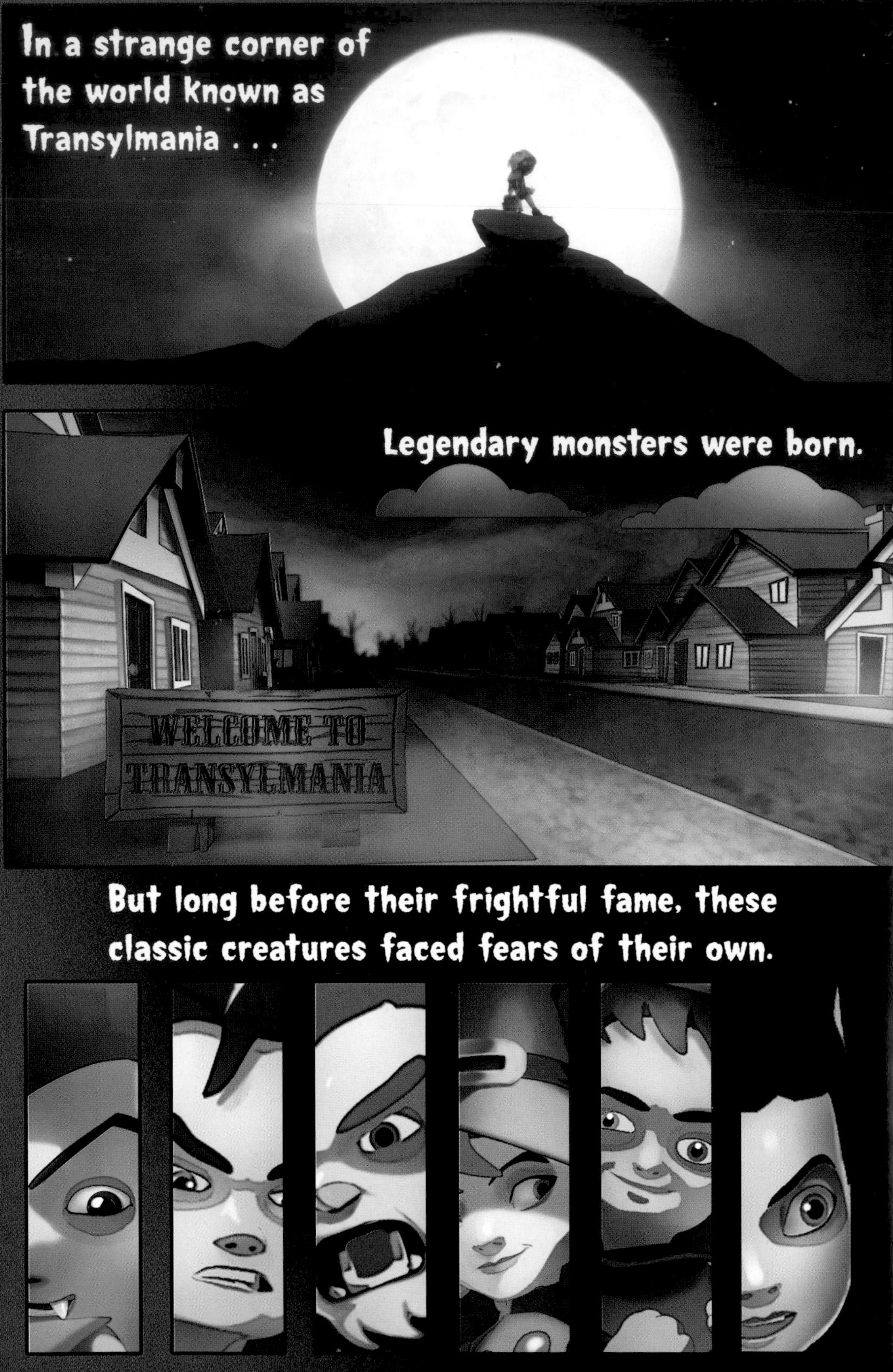
In a strange corner of the world known as Transylmania . . .
Legendary monsters were born.
WELCOME TO TRANSYLMANIA
But long before their frightful fame, these classic creatures faced fears of their own.

To take on terrifying teachers and homework horrors, they formed the most fearsome friendship on Earth . . .

Mighty Mighty MONSTERS

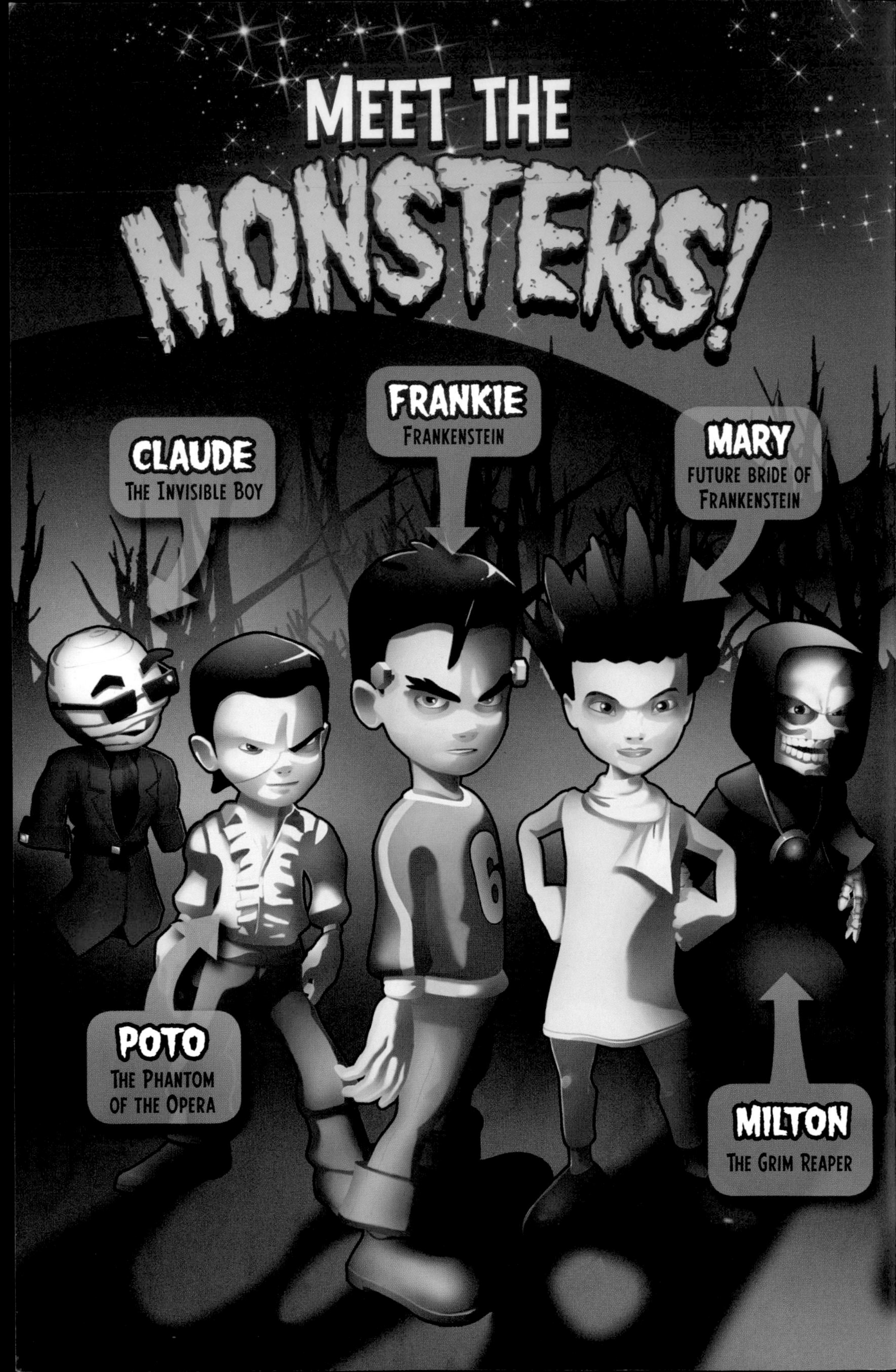
MEET THE
MONSTERS!
CLAUDE
THE INVISIBLE BOY
FRANKIE
FRANKENSTEIN
MARY
FUTURE BRIDE OF FRANKENSTEIN
POTO
THE PHANTOM OF THE OPERA
MILTON
THE GRIM REAPER

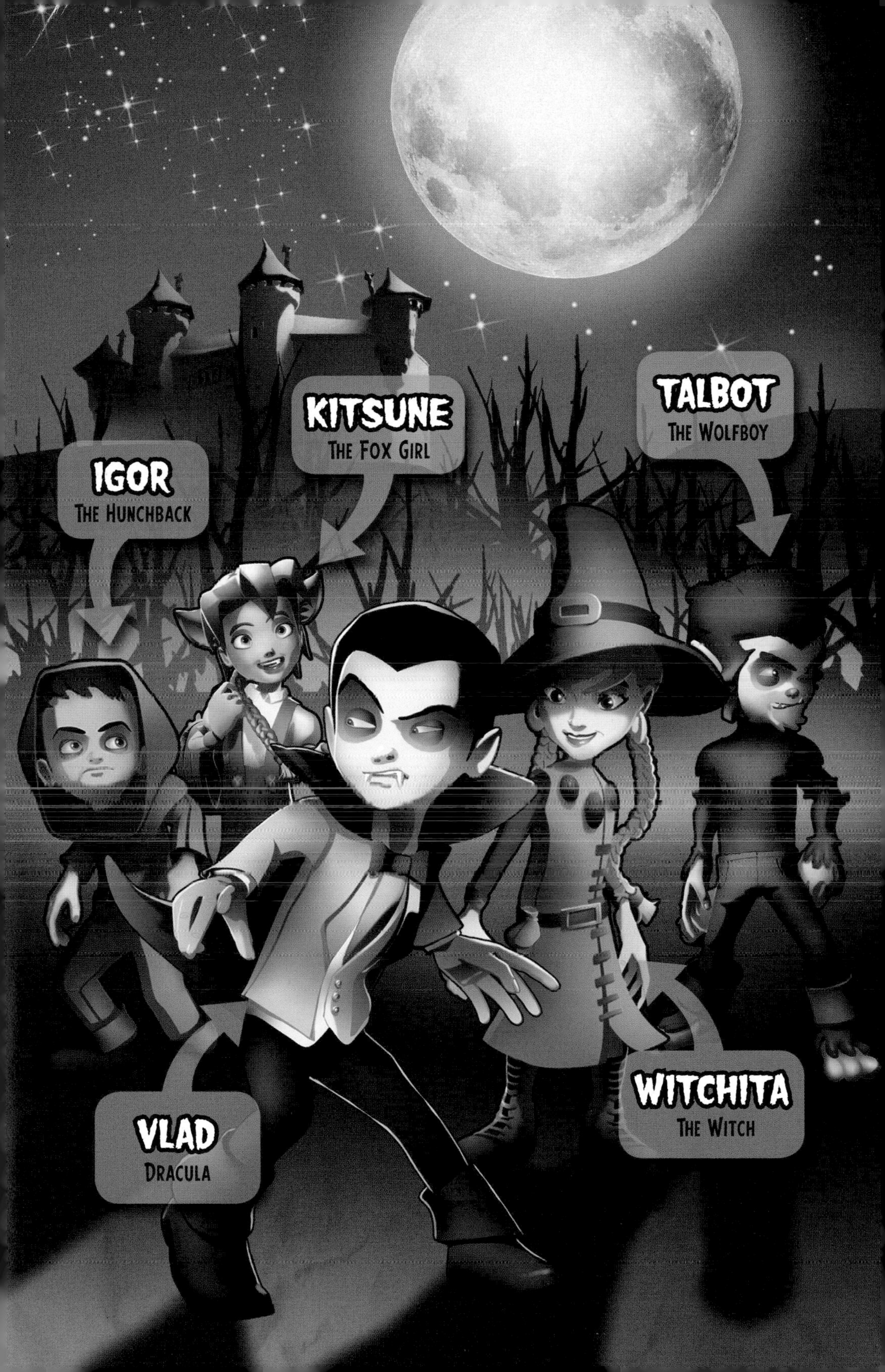
IGOR
THE HUNCHBACK
KITSUNE
THE FOX GIRL
TALBOT
THE WOLFBOY
VLAD
DRACULA
WITCHITA
THE WITCH

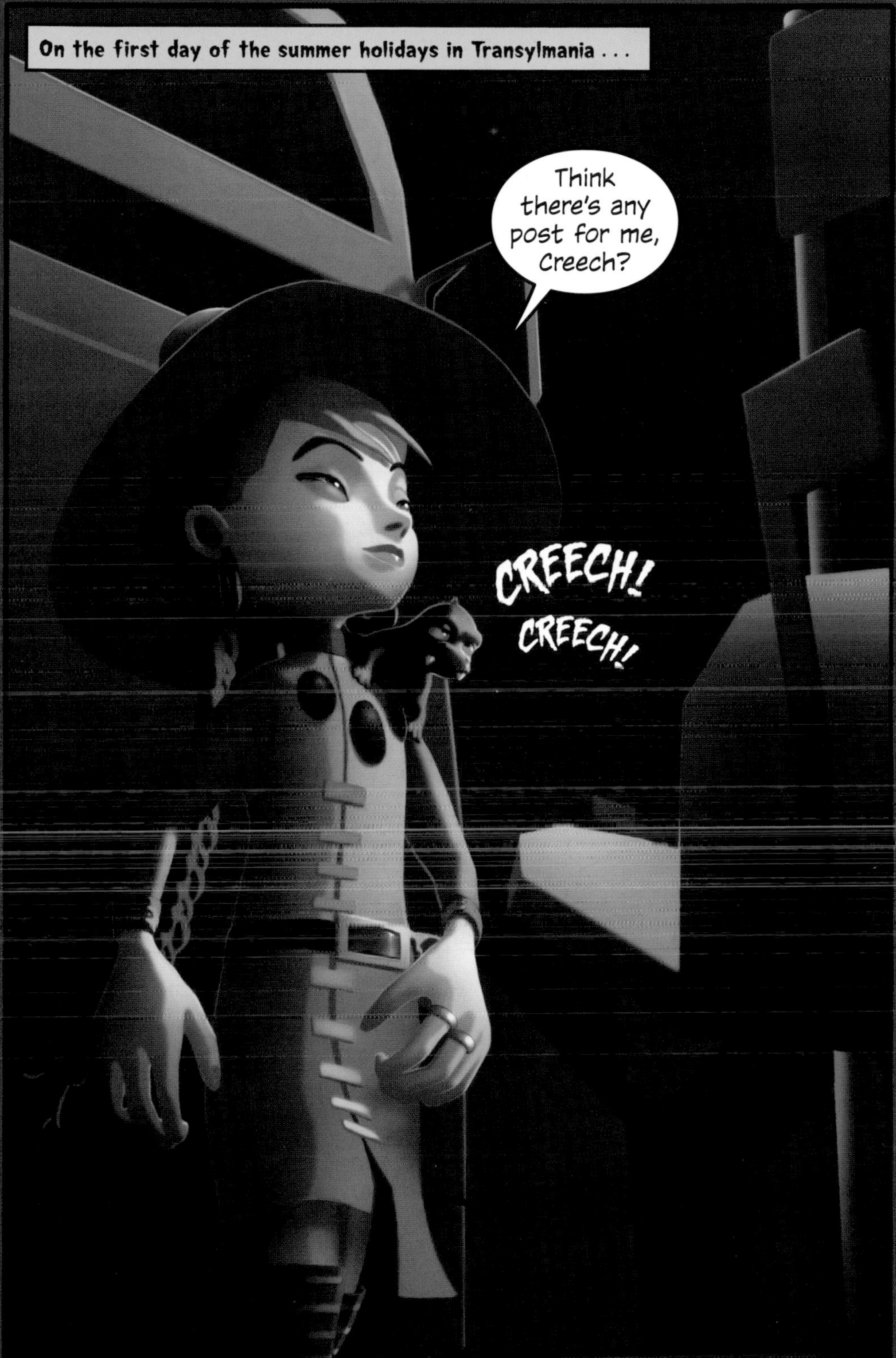
On the first day of the summer holidays in Transylmania . . .
Think there's any post for me, Creech?
CREECH!
CREECH!

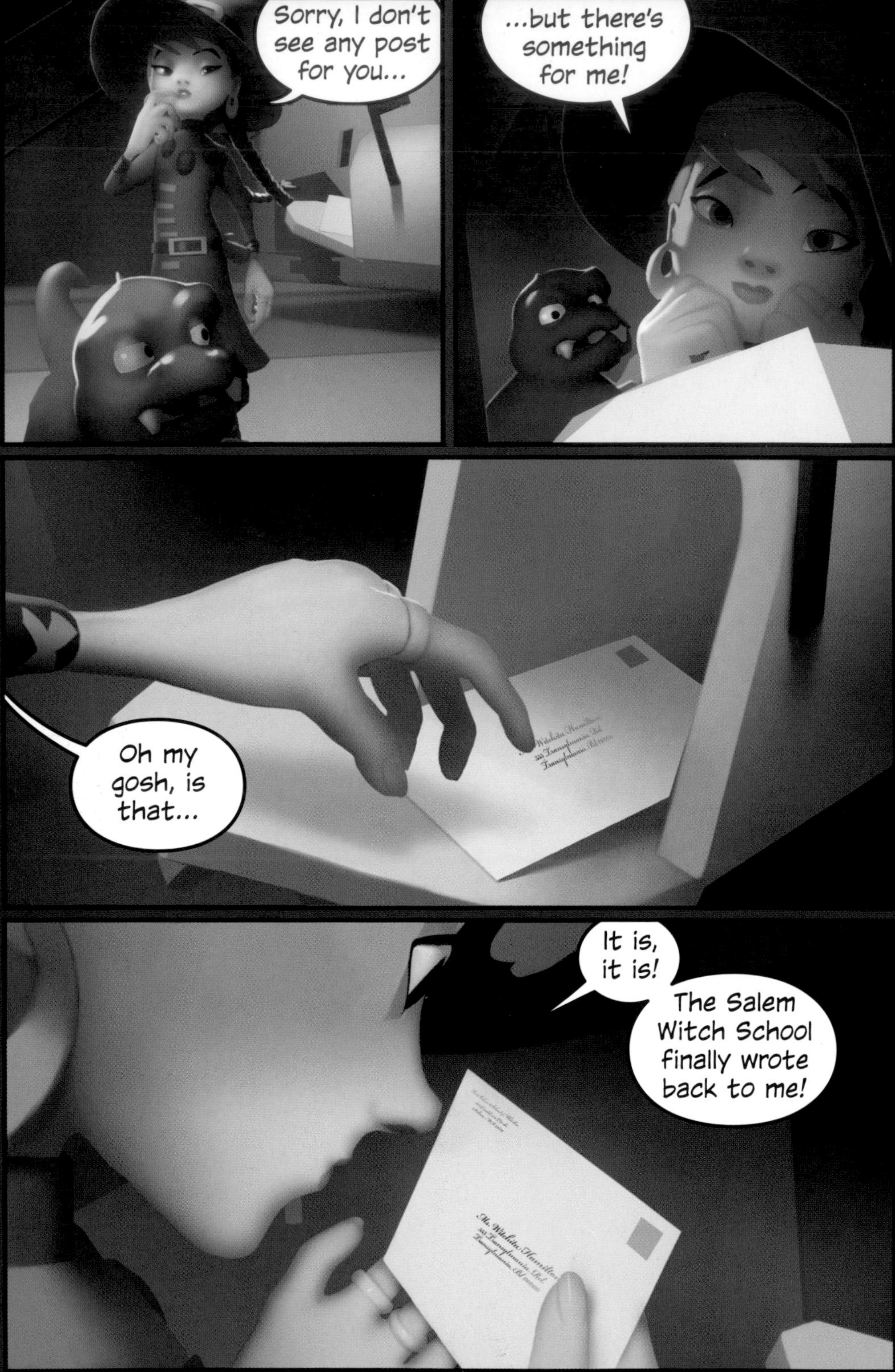
Sorry, I don't see any post for you...
...but there's something for me!
Oh my gosh, is that...
It is, it is!
The Salem Witch School finally wrote back to me!

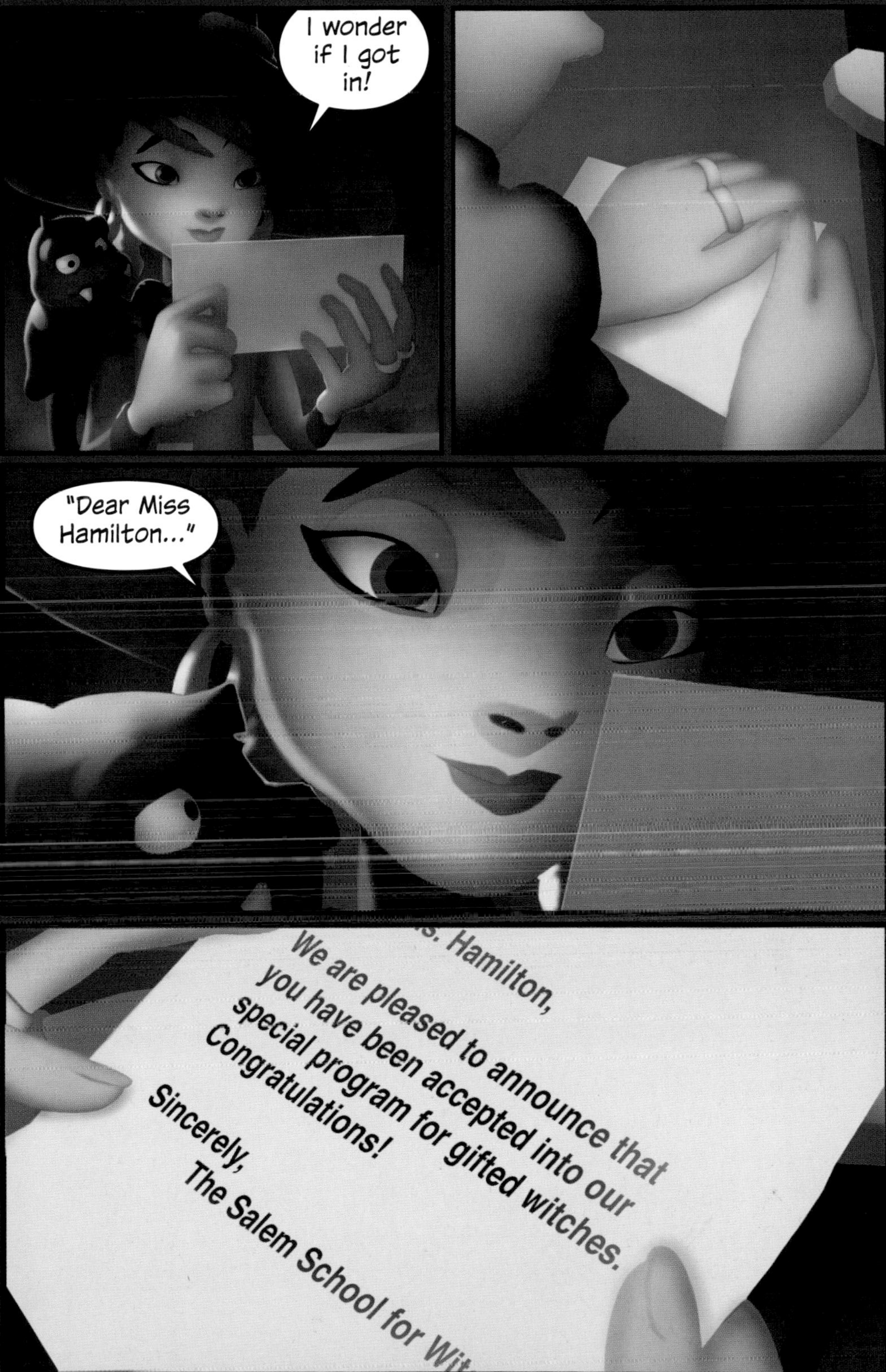
I wonder if I got in!
"Dear Miss Hamilton..."
s. Hamilton,
We are pleased to announce that
you have been accepted into our
special program for gifted witches.
Congratulations!
Sincerely,
The Salem School for Wi

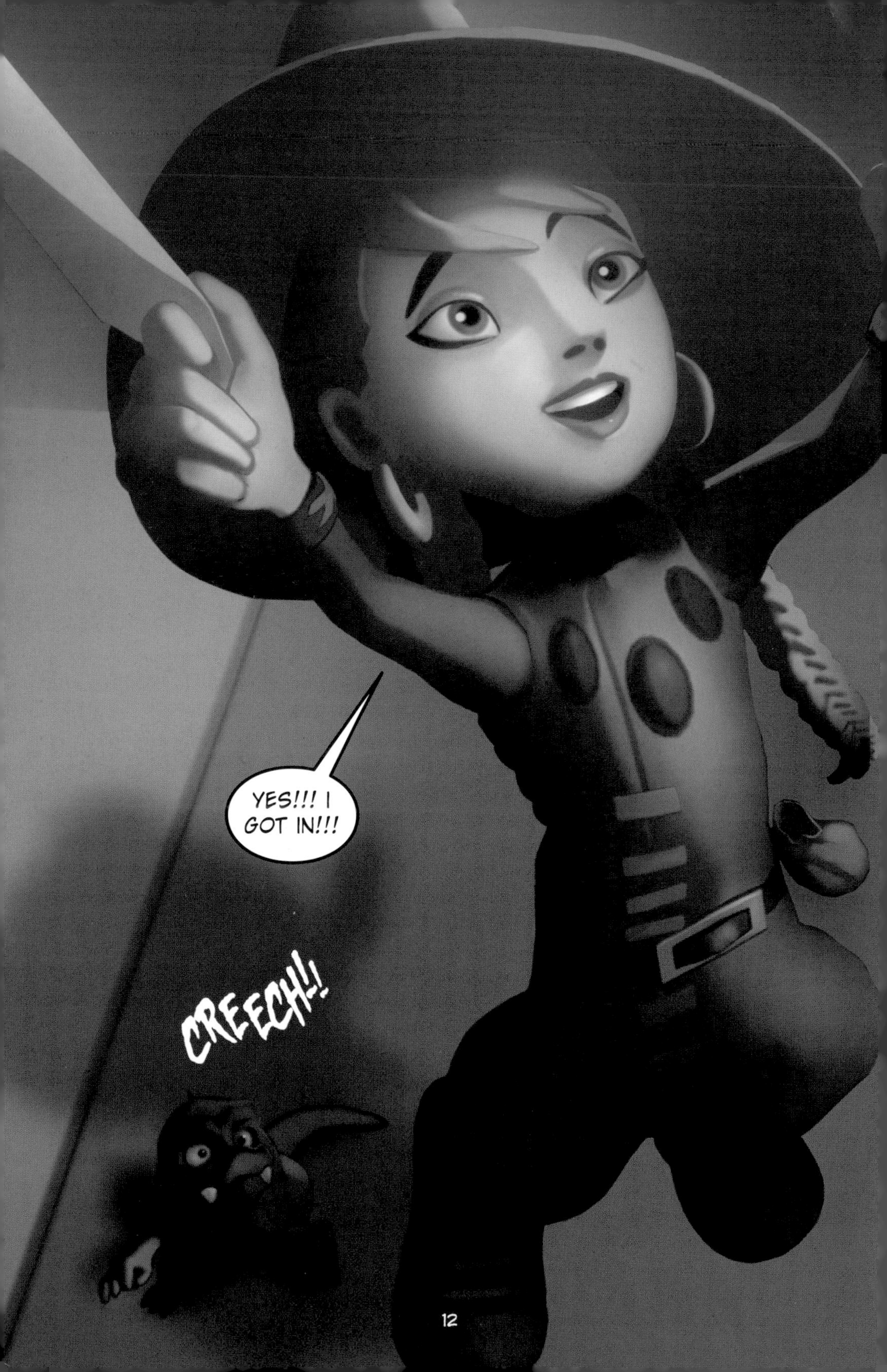
YES!!! I GOT IN!!!
CREECH!!

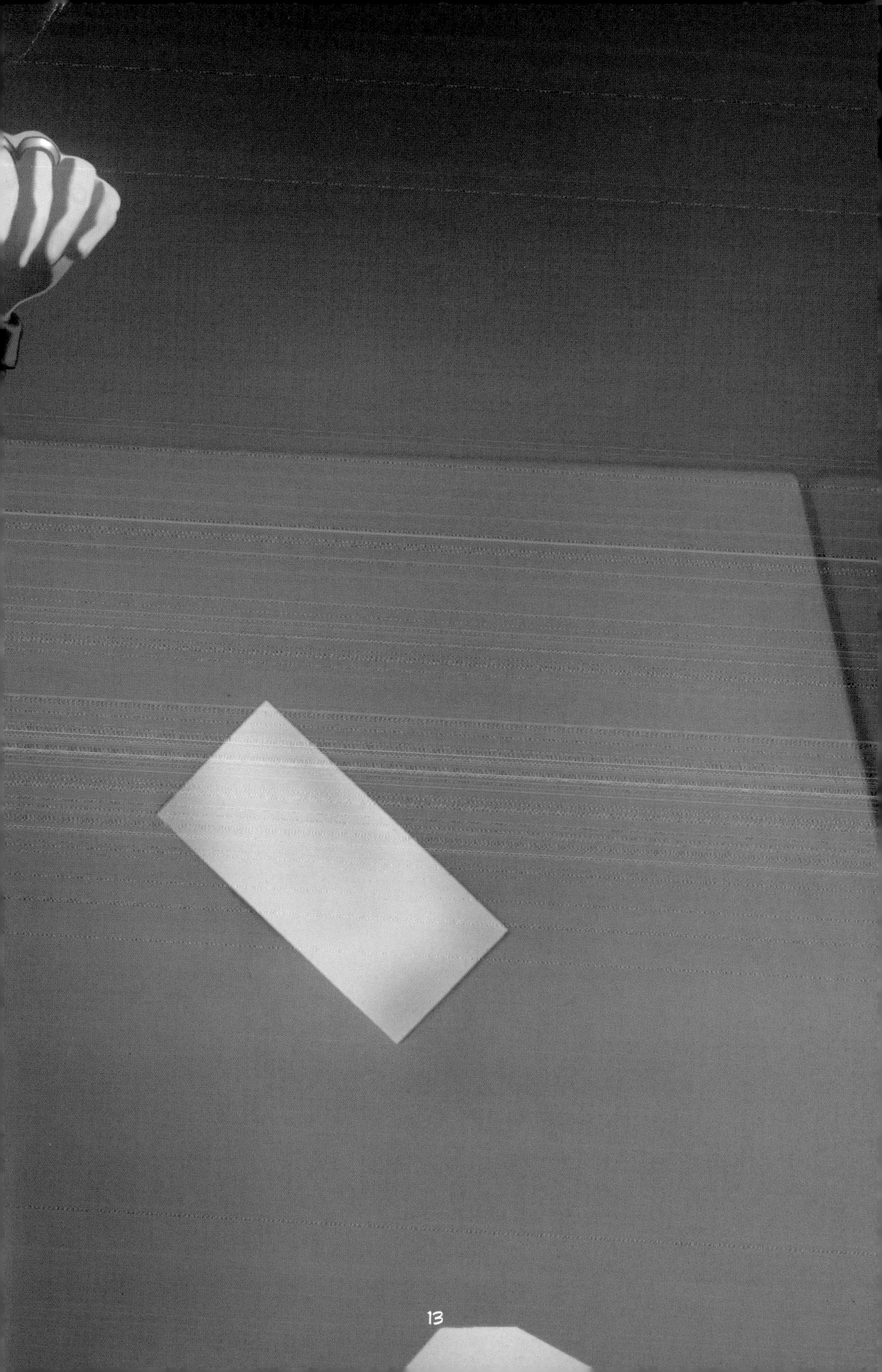

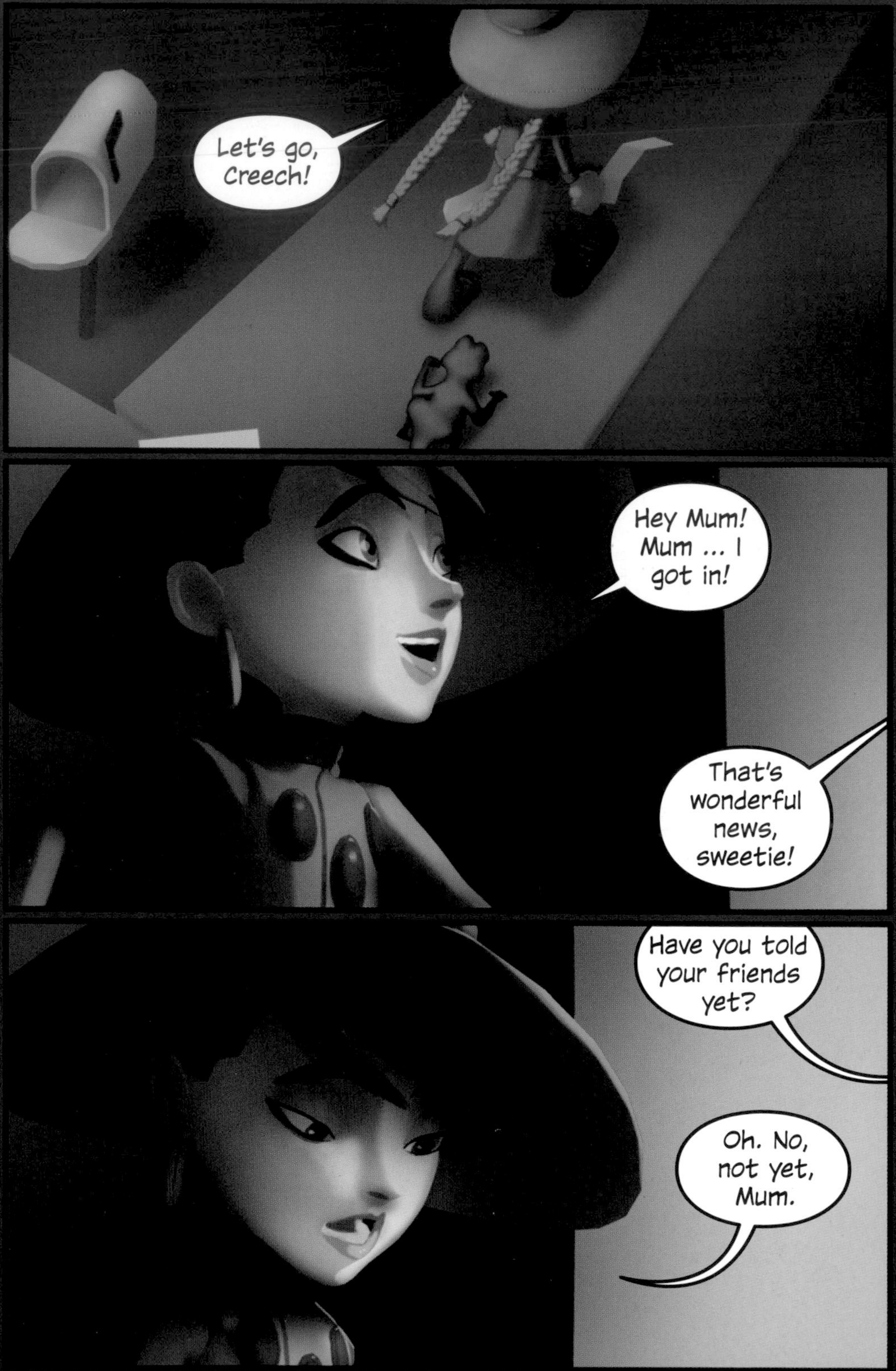
Let's go, Creech!
Hey Mum! Mum ... I got in!
That's wonderful news, sweetie!
Have you told your friends yet?
Oh. No, not yet, Mum.

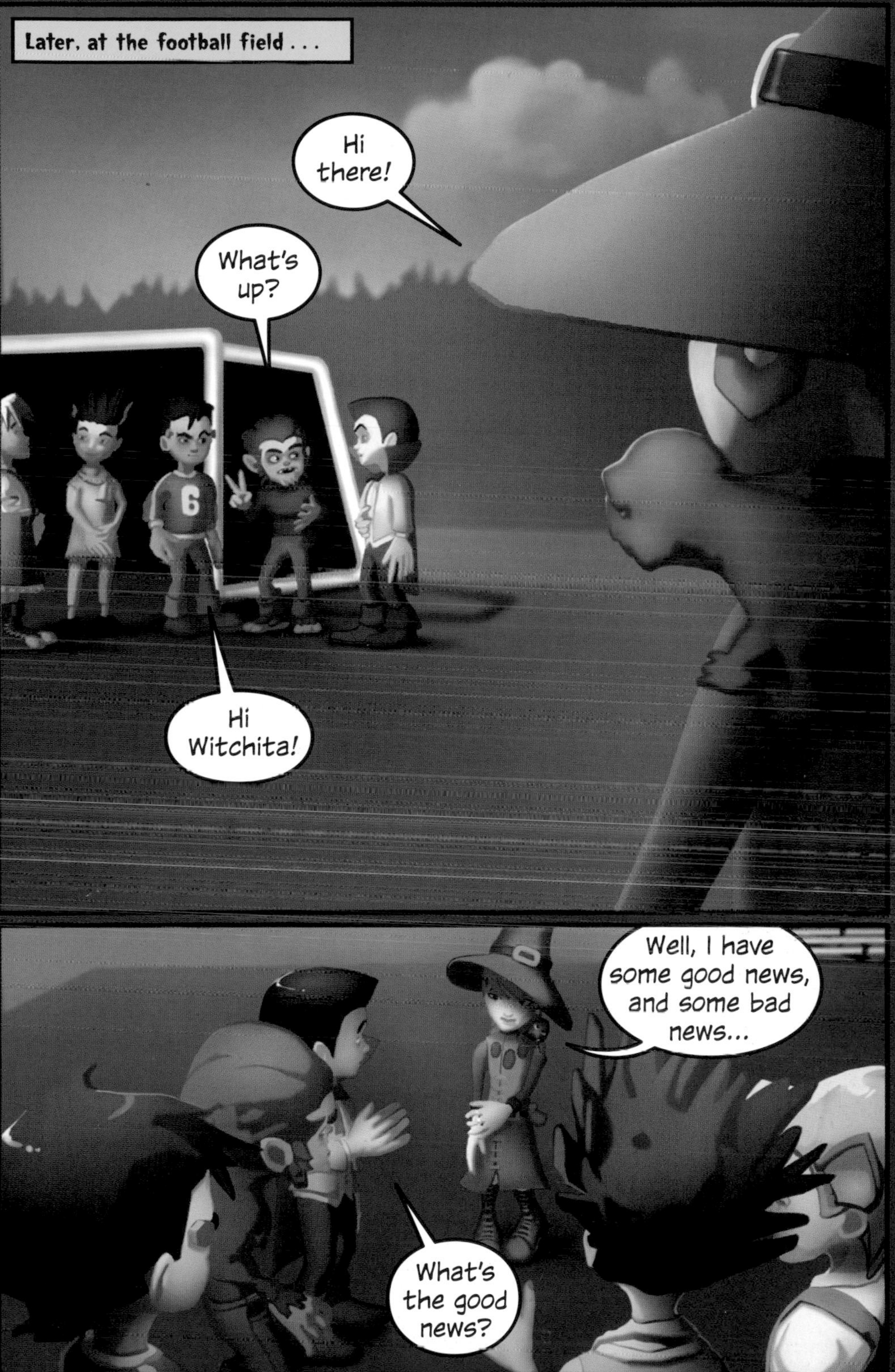
Later, at the football field . . .
Hi there!
What's up?
Hi Witchita!
Well, I have some good news, and some bad news...
What's the good news?

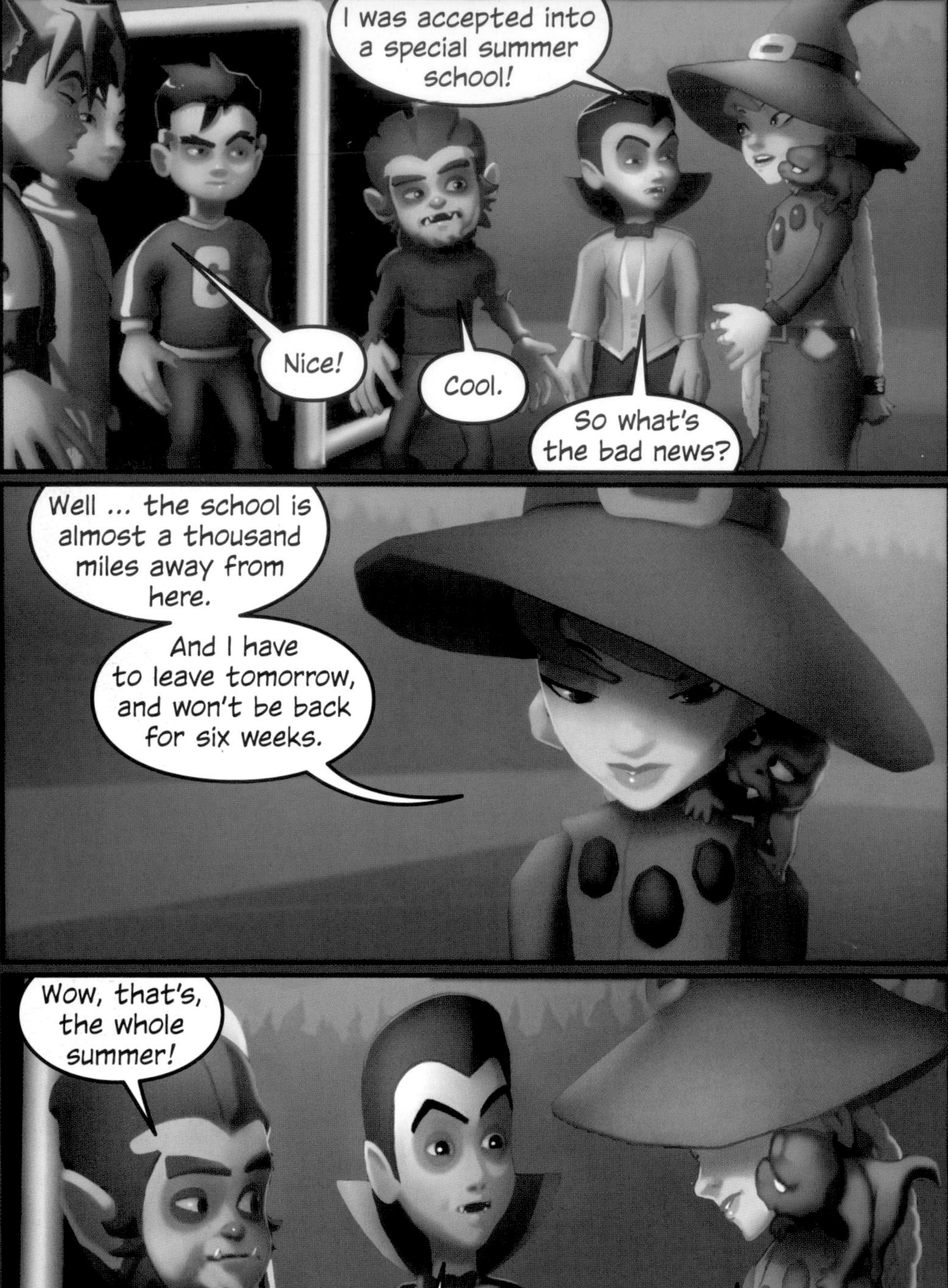
I was accepted into a special summer school!
Nice!
Cool.
So what's the bad news?
Well ... the school is almost a thousand miles away from here.
And I have to leave tomorrow, and won't be back for six weeks.
Wow, that's, the whole summer!
Yeah – we wouldn't see you until September!
I know, Vlad. But I really want to go.

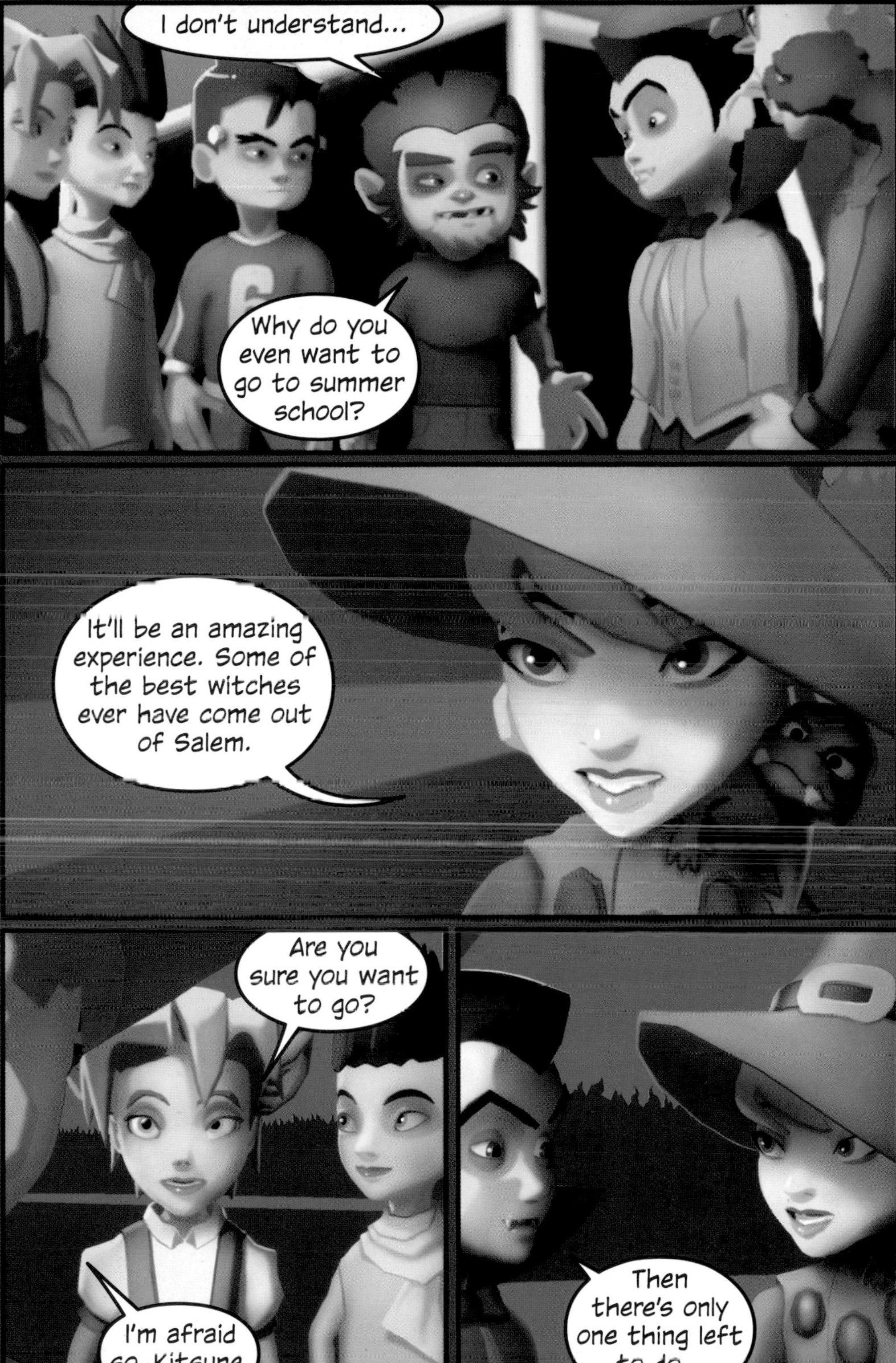
I don't understand...
Why do you even want to go to summer school?
It'll be an amazing experience. Some of the best witches ever have come out of Salem.
Are you sure you want to go?
I'm afraid so, Kitsune.
Then there's only one thing left to do...

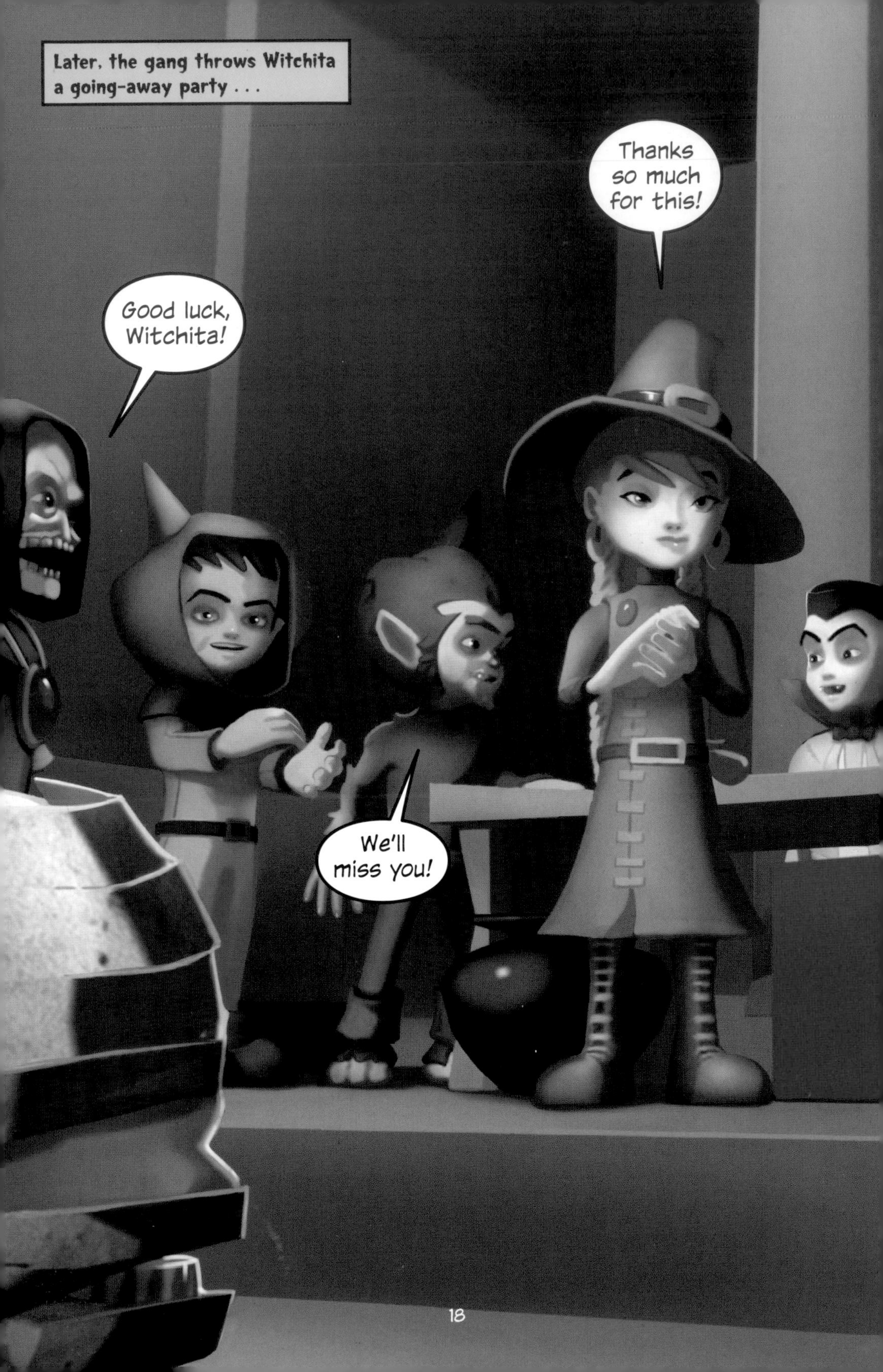
Later, the gang throws Witchita a going-away party . . .
Good luck, Witchita!
Thanks so much for this!
We'll miss you!

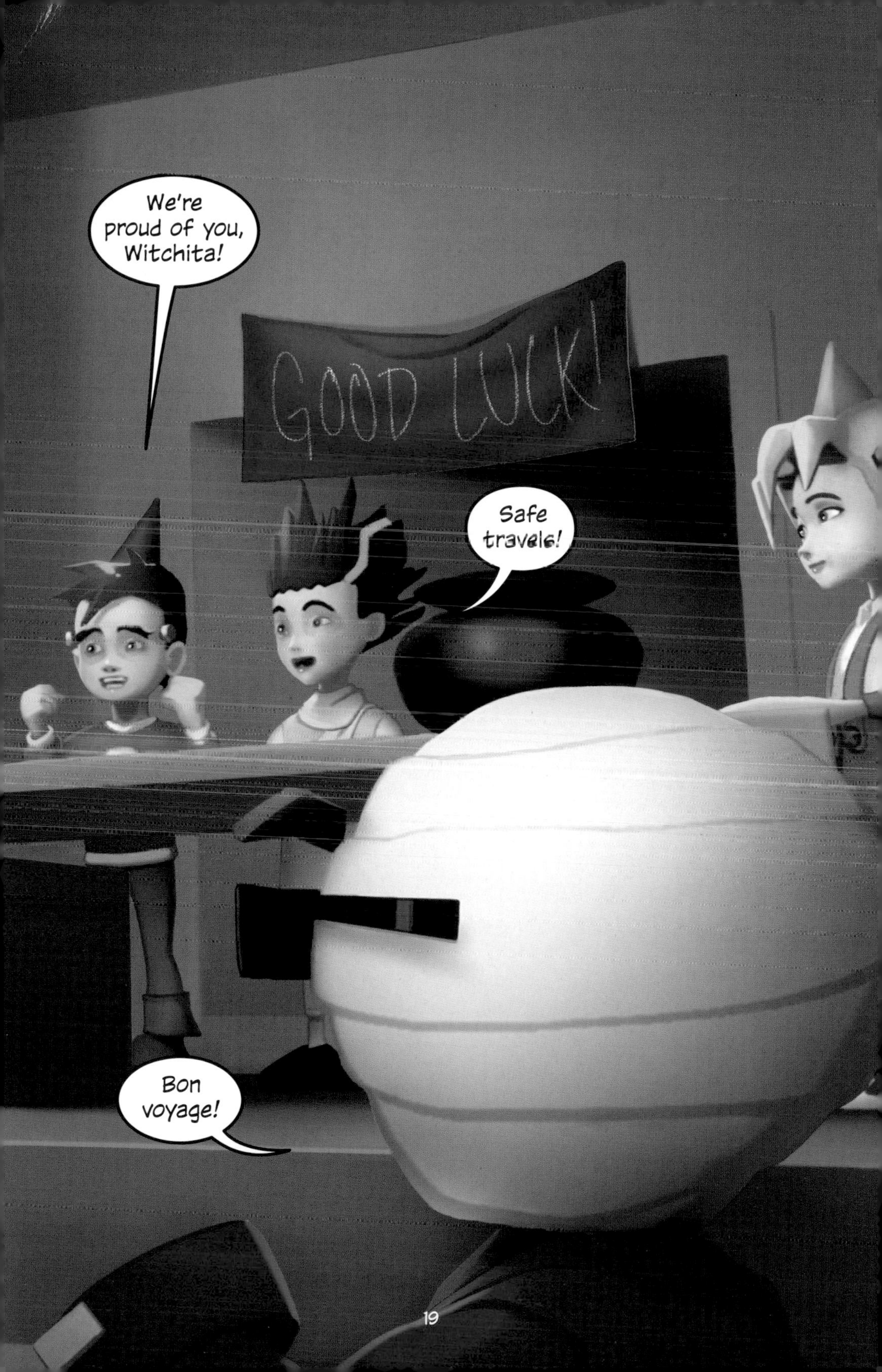
We're proud of you, Witchita!
GOOD LUCK!
Safe travels!
Bon voyage!

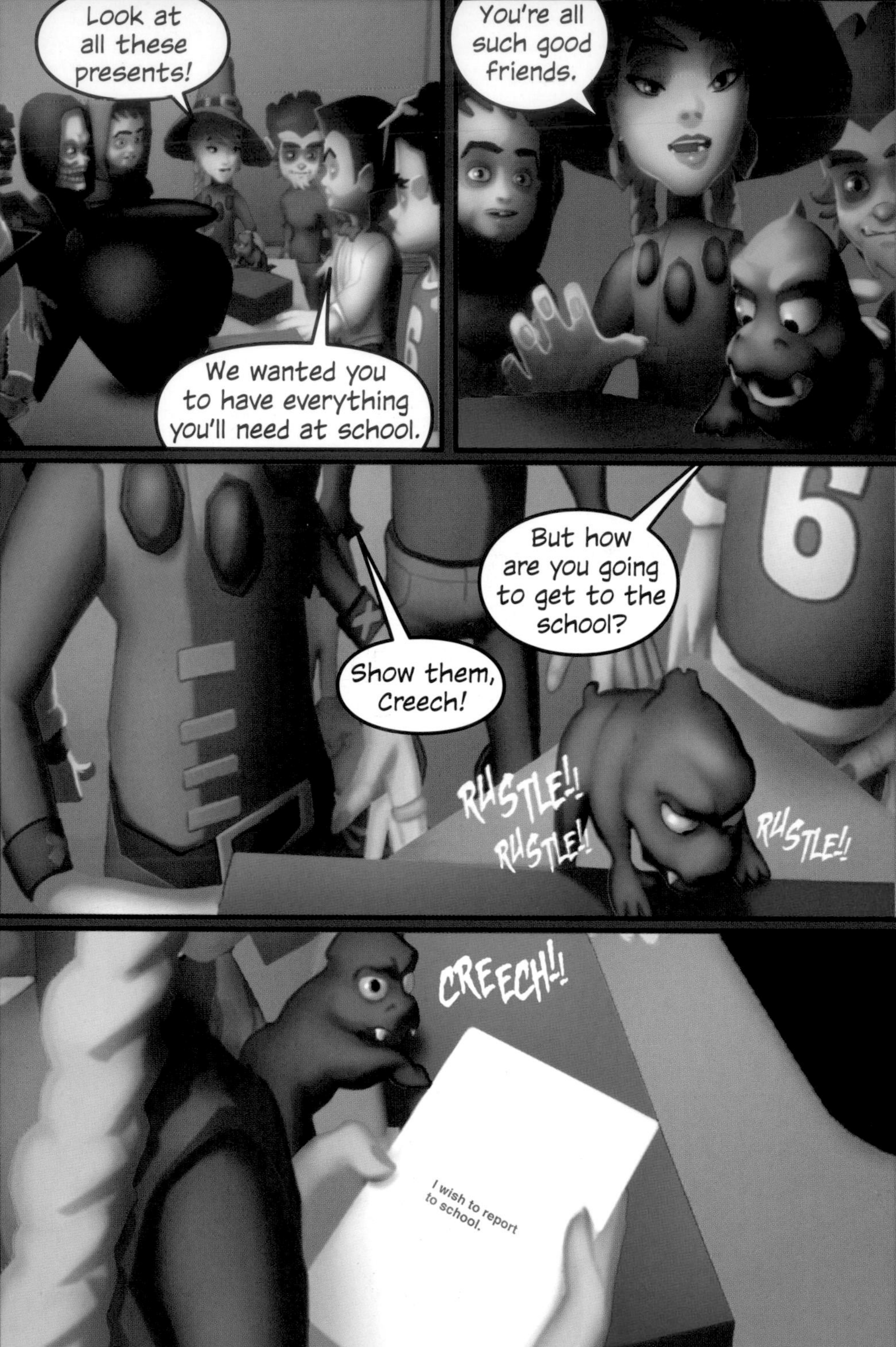
Look at all these presents!
We wanted you to have everything you'll need at school.
You're all such good friends.
But how are you going to get to the school?
Show them, Creech!
RUSTLE!!
RUSTLE!!
RUSTLE!!
CREECH!!
I wish to report to school.

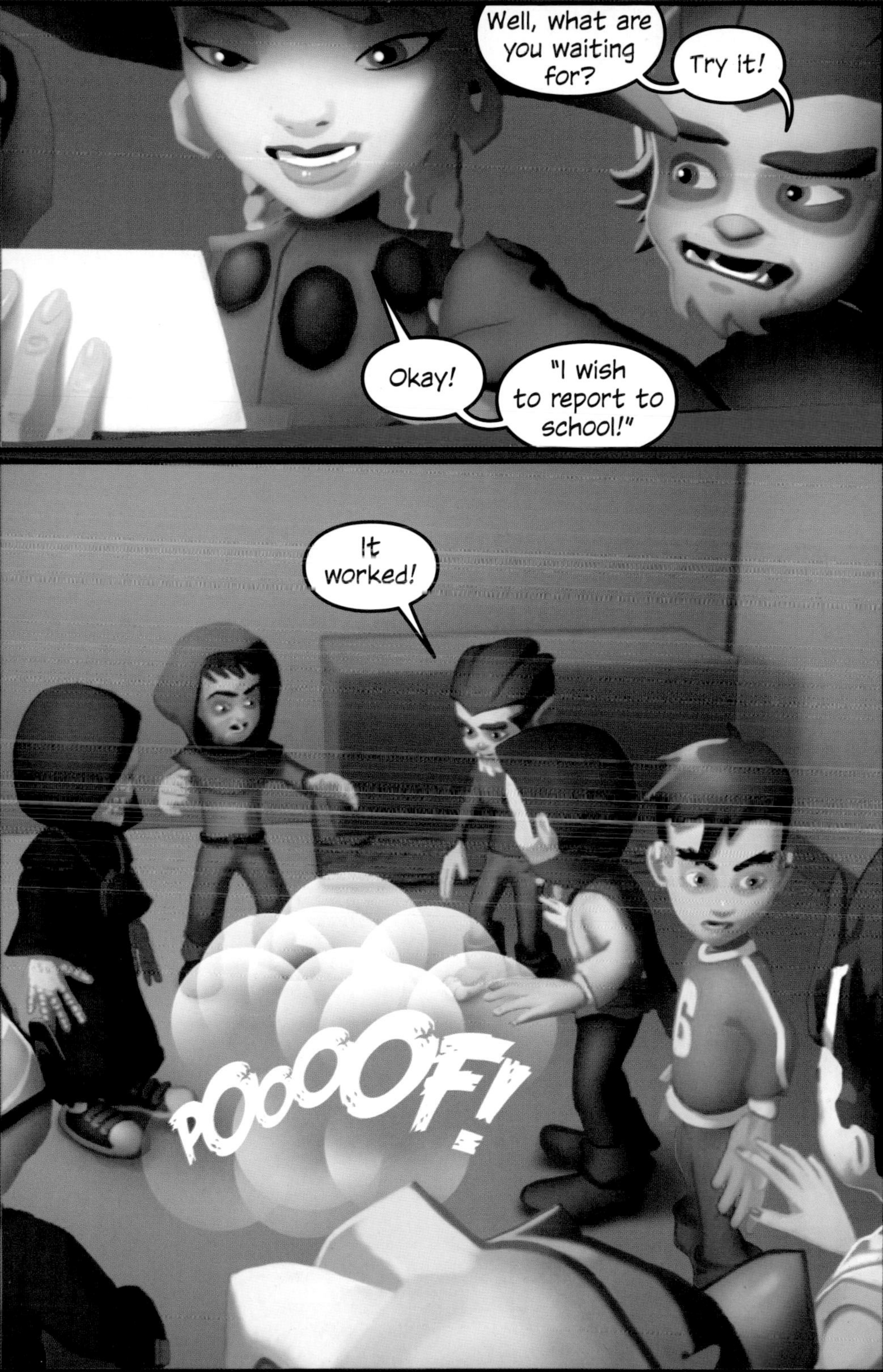
Well, what are you waiting for?
Try it!
Okay!
"I wish to report to school!"
It worked!
POOOOF!

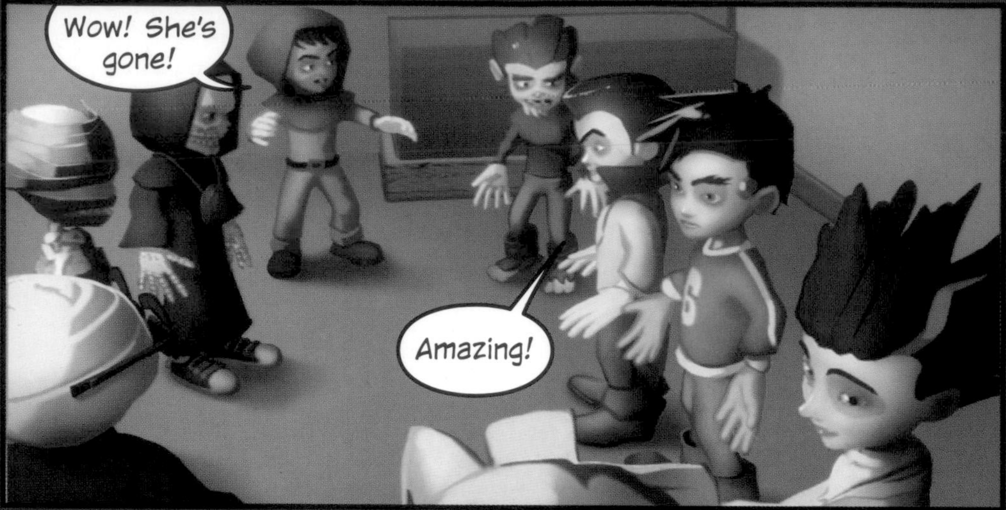
Wow! She's gone!
Amazing!

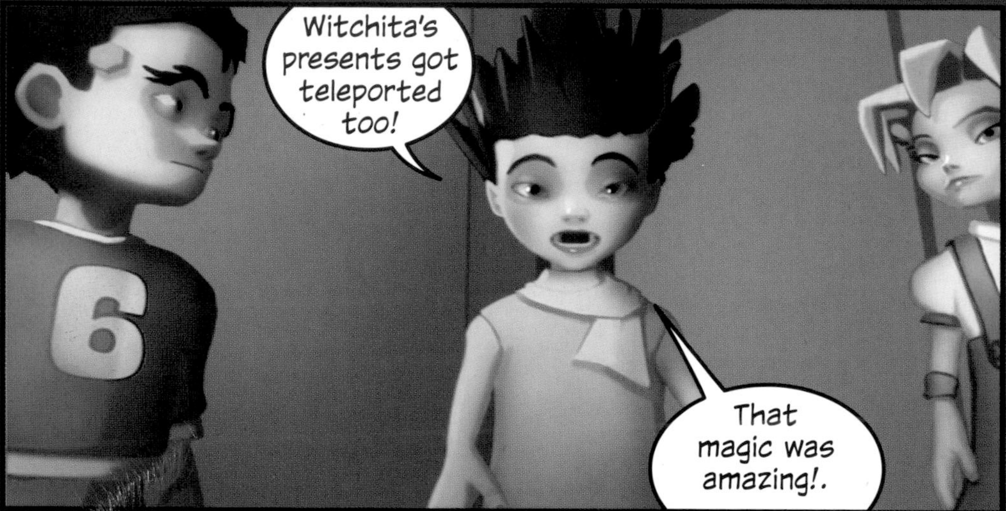
Witchita's presents got teleported too!
That magic was amazing!.

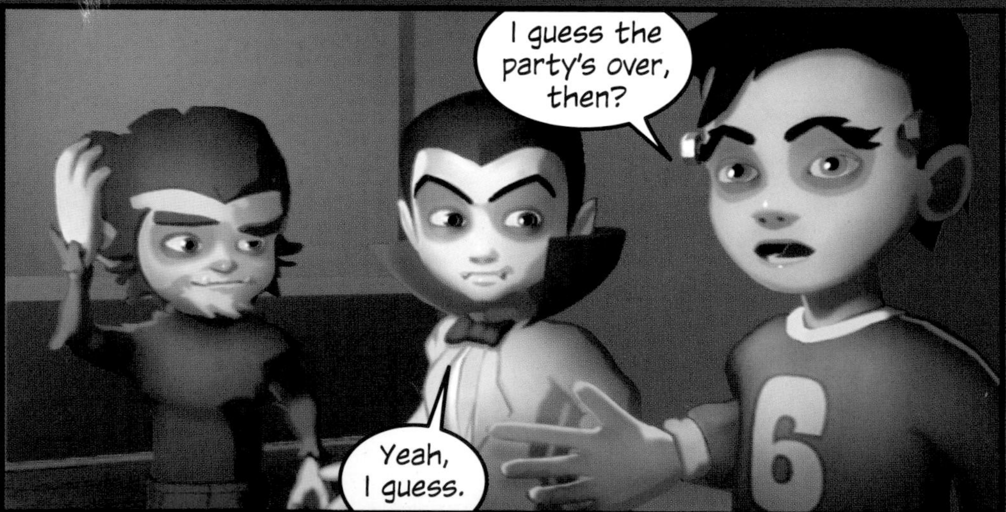
I guess the party's over, then?
Yeah, I guess.

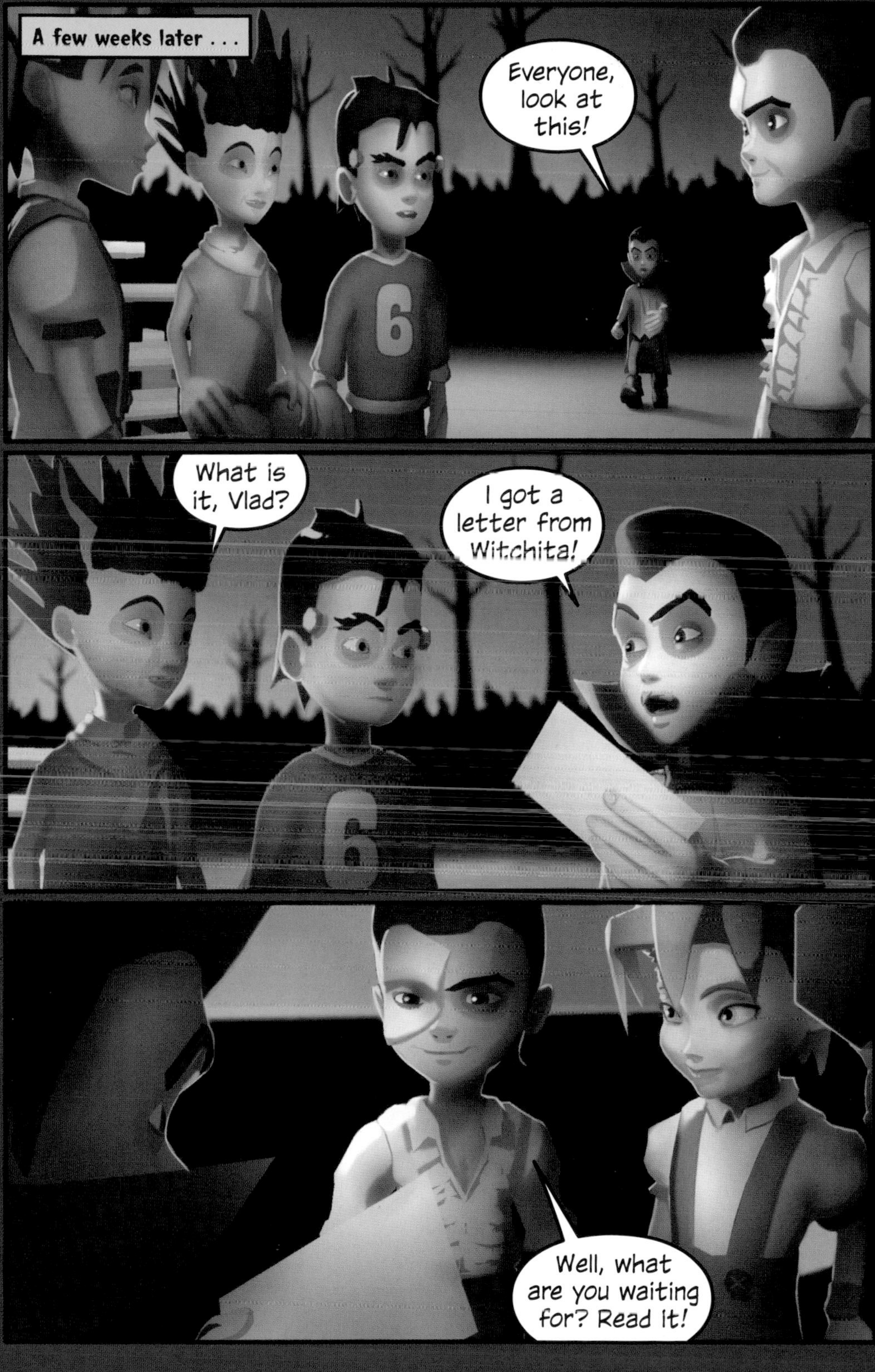
A few weeks later . . .
Everyone, look at this!
What is it, Vlad?
I got a letter from Witchita!
Well, what are you waiting for? Read it!

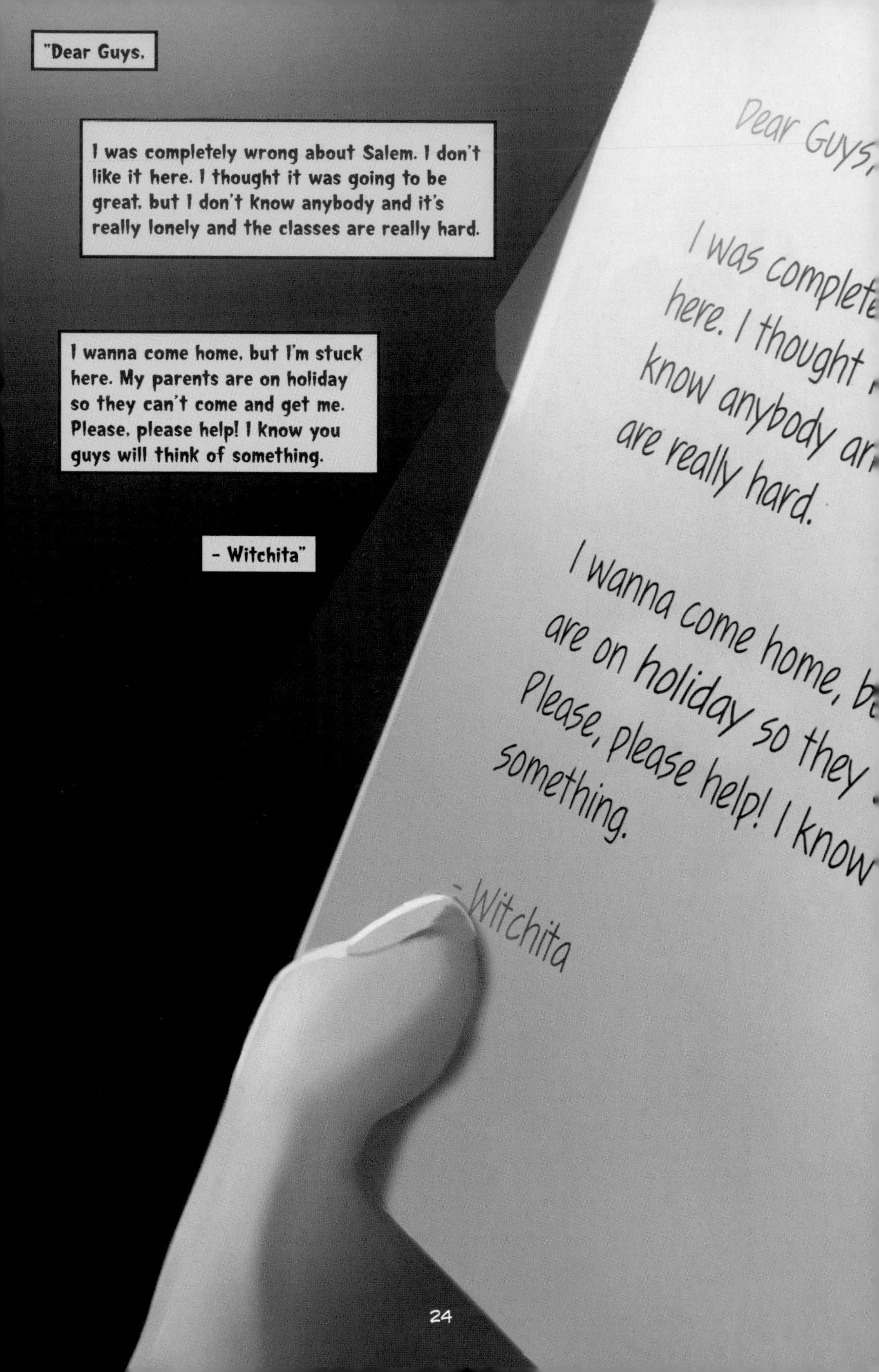
"Dear Guys,
I was completely wrong about Salem. I don't like it here. I thought it was going to be great, but I don't know anybody and it's really lonely and the classes are really hard.
I wanna come home, but I'm stuck here. My parents are on holiday so they can't come and get me. Please, please help! I know you guys will think of something.
- Witchita"
Dear Guys,
I was
here. I thought
know anybody
are really hard.
I wanna come home,
are on holiday so they
Please, please help! I know
something.
- Witchita

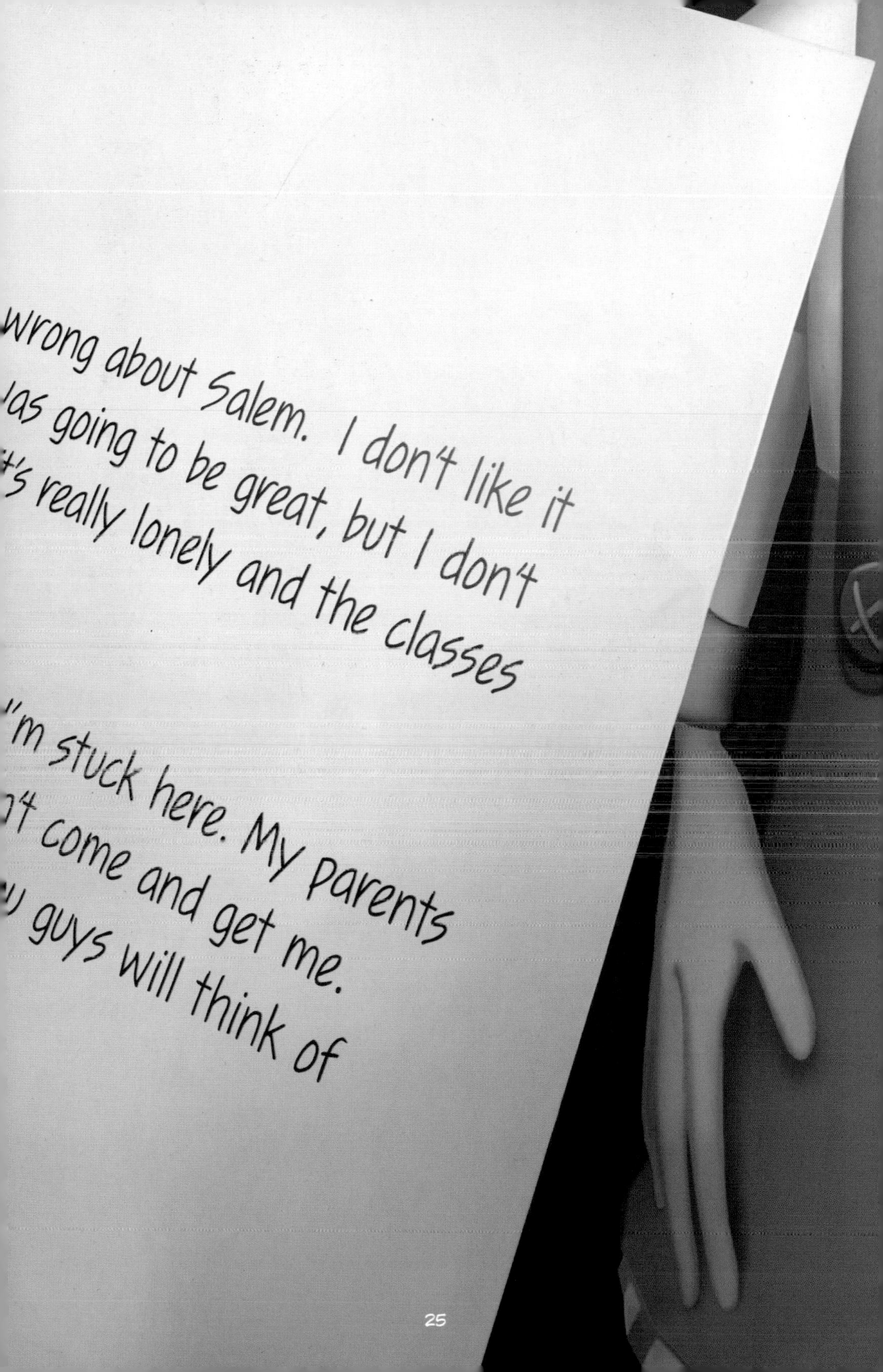
wrong about Salem. I don't like it
as going to be great, but I don't
's really lonely and the classes
'm stuck here. My parents
't come and get me.
guys will think of

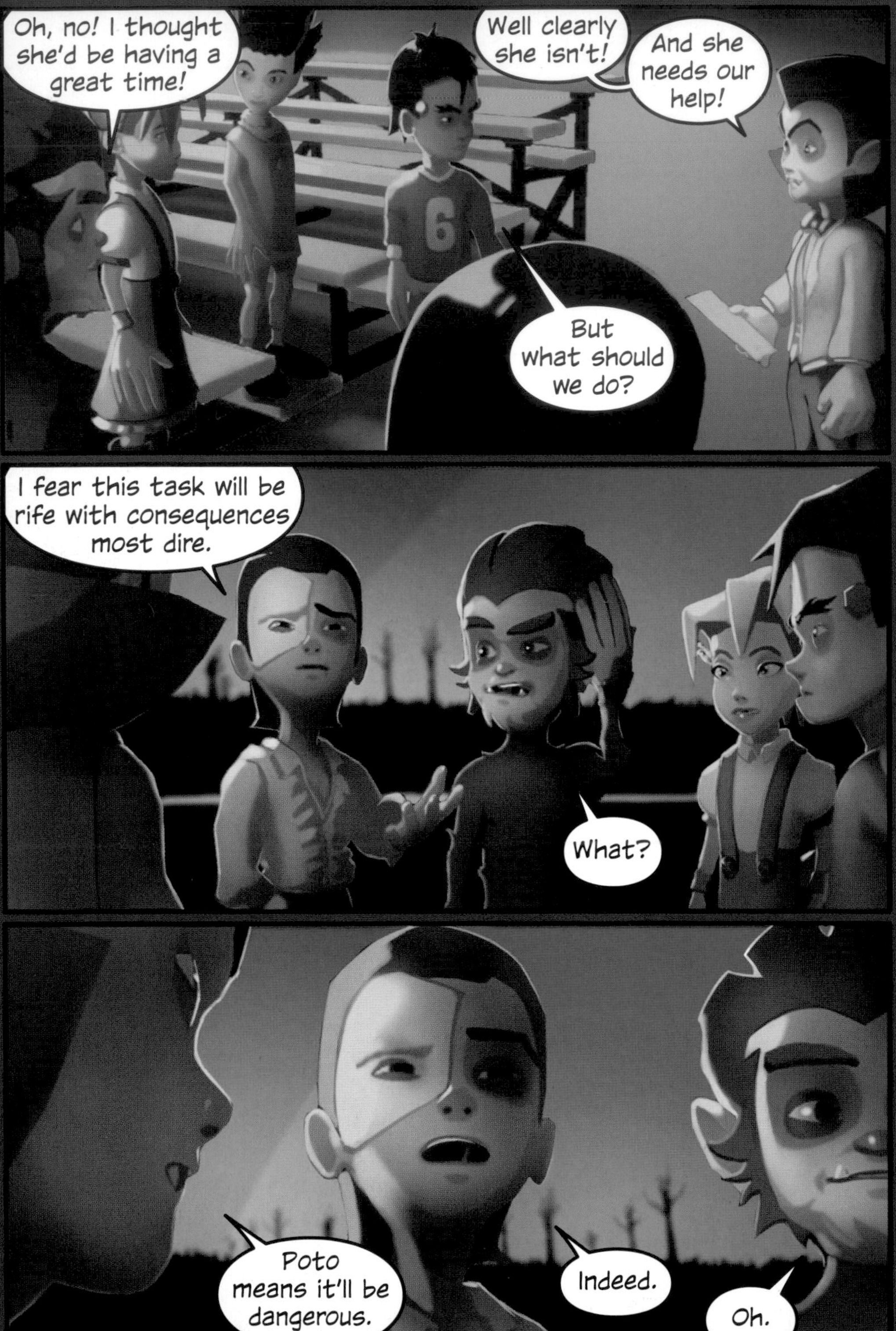
Oh, no! I thought she'd be having a great time!
Well clearly she isn't!
And she needs our help!
But what should we do?
I fear this task will be rife with consequences most dire.
What?
Poto means it'll be dangerous.
Indeed.
Oh.

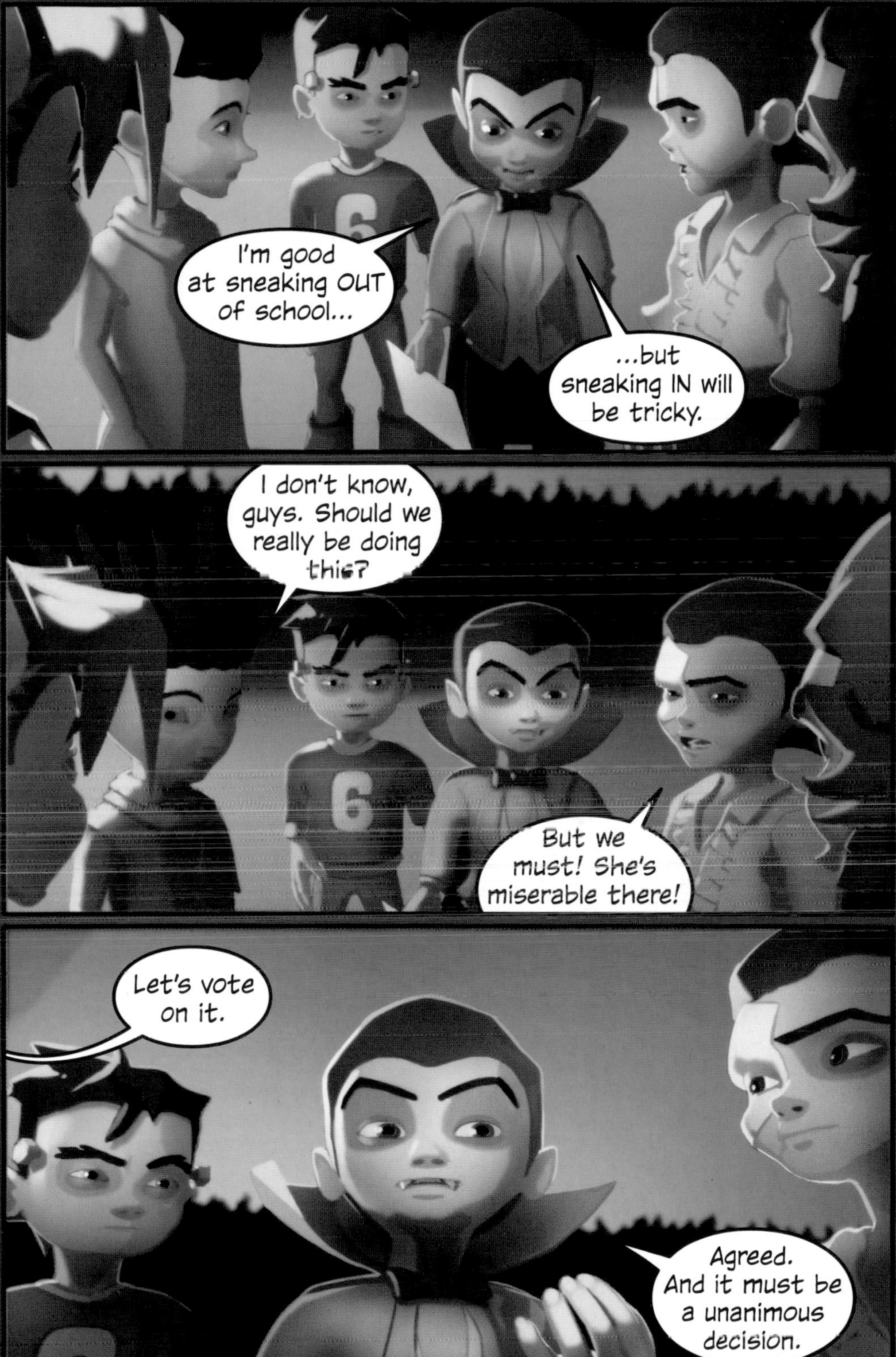
I'm good at sneaking OUT of school...
...but sneaking IN will be tricky.
I don't know, guys. Should we really be doing this?
But we must! She's miserable there!
Let's vote on it.
Agreed. And it must be a unanimous decision.

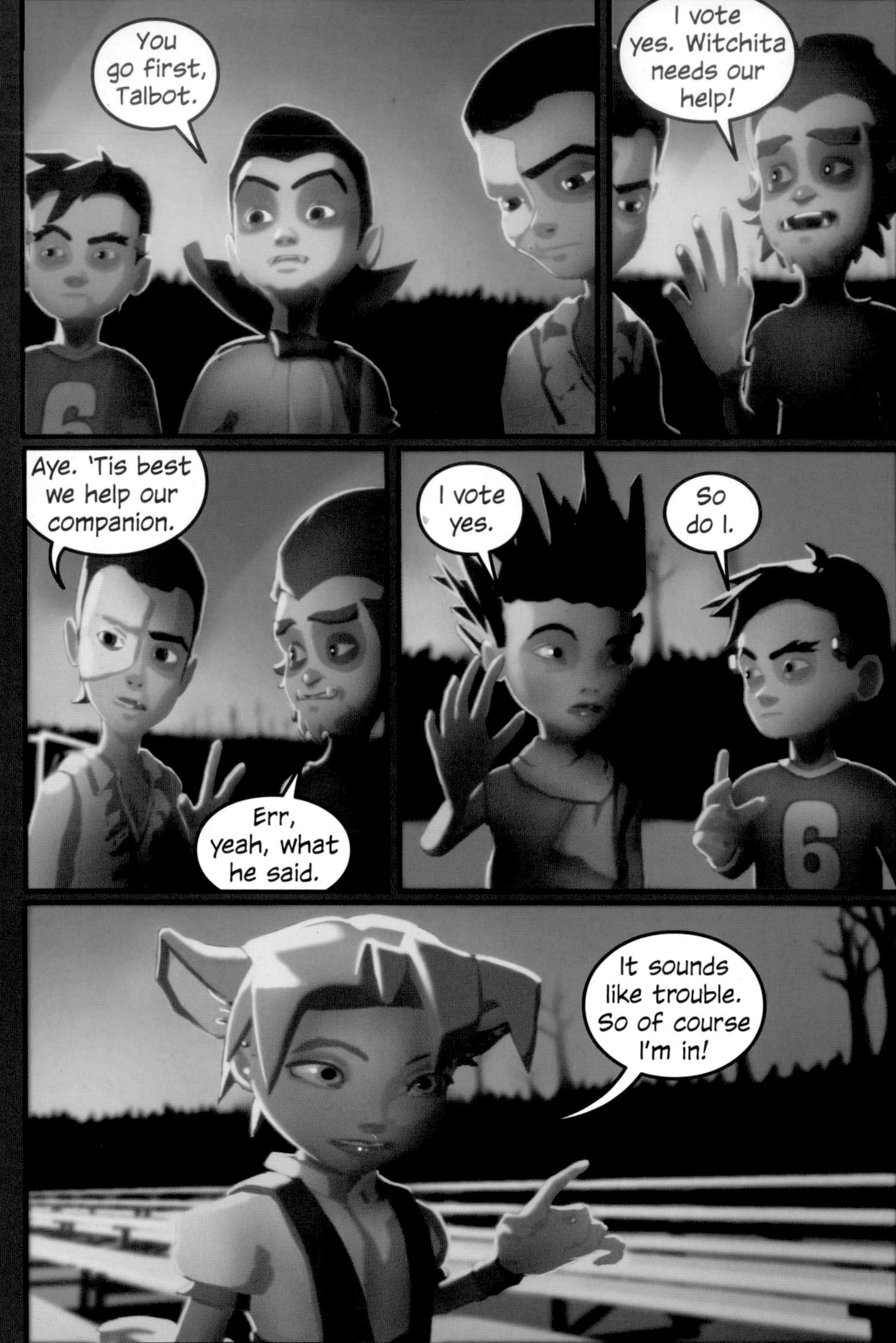
You go first, Talbot.
I vote yes. Witchita needs our help!
Aye. 'Tis best we help our companion.
Err, yeah, what he said.
I vote yes.
So do I.
It sounds like trouble. So of course I'm in!

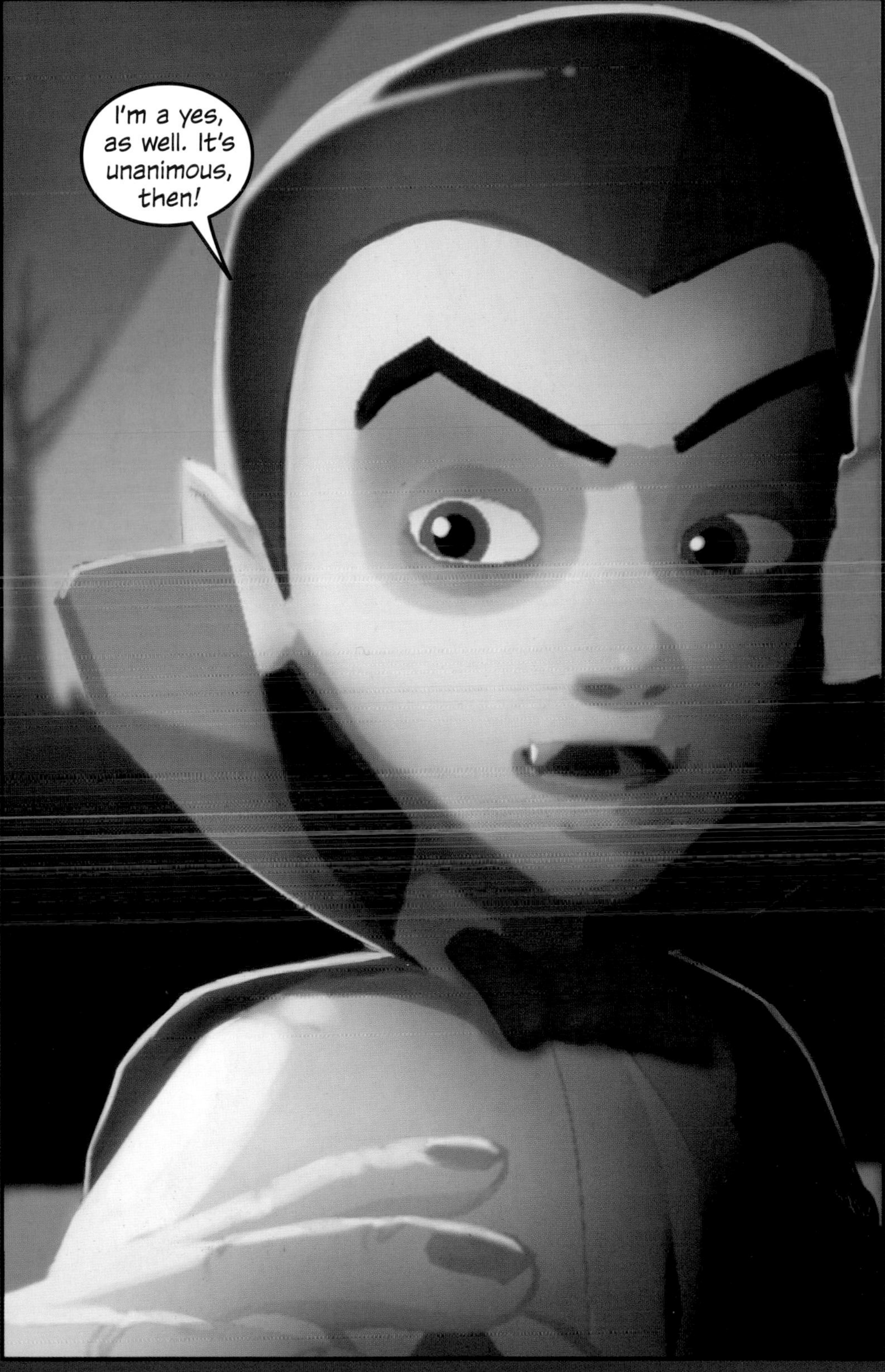
I'm a yes, as well. It's unanimous, then!

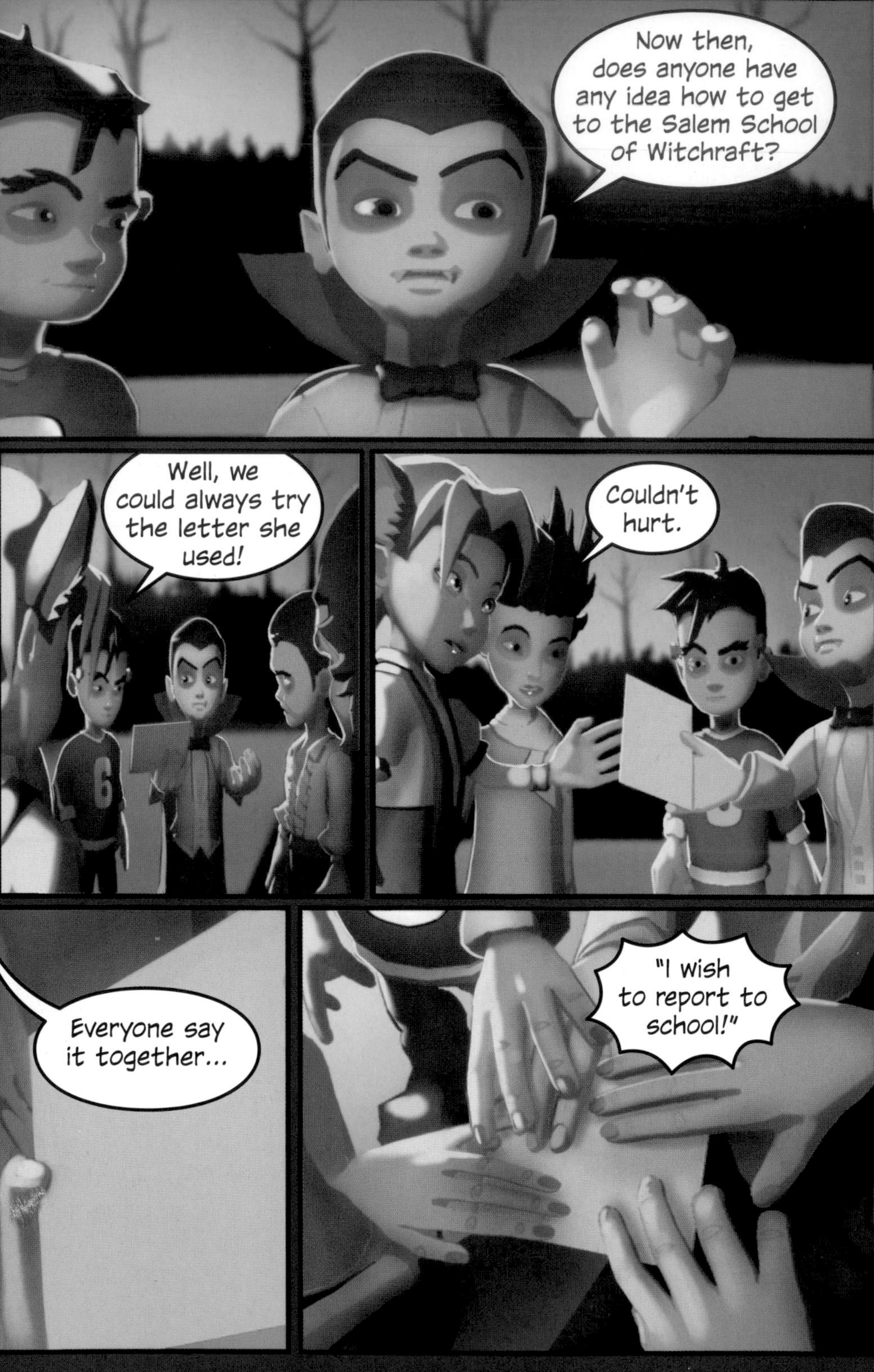
Now then, does anyone have any idea how to get to the Salem School of Witchcraft?
Well, we could always try the letter she used!
Couldn't hurt.
Everyone say it together...
"I wish to report to school!"

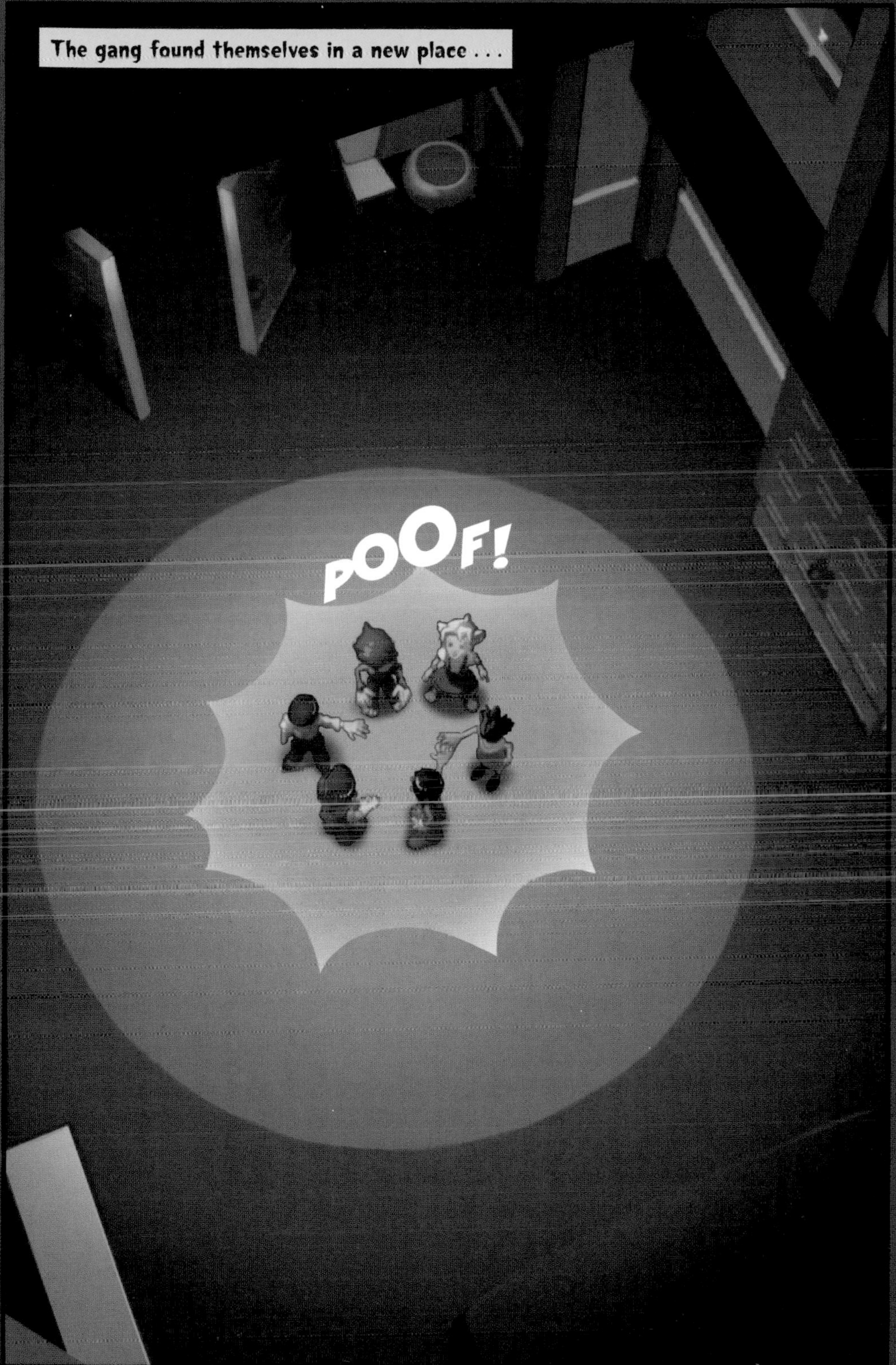
The gang found themselves in a new place . . .
POOF!

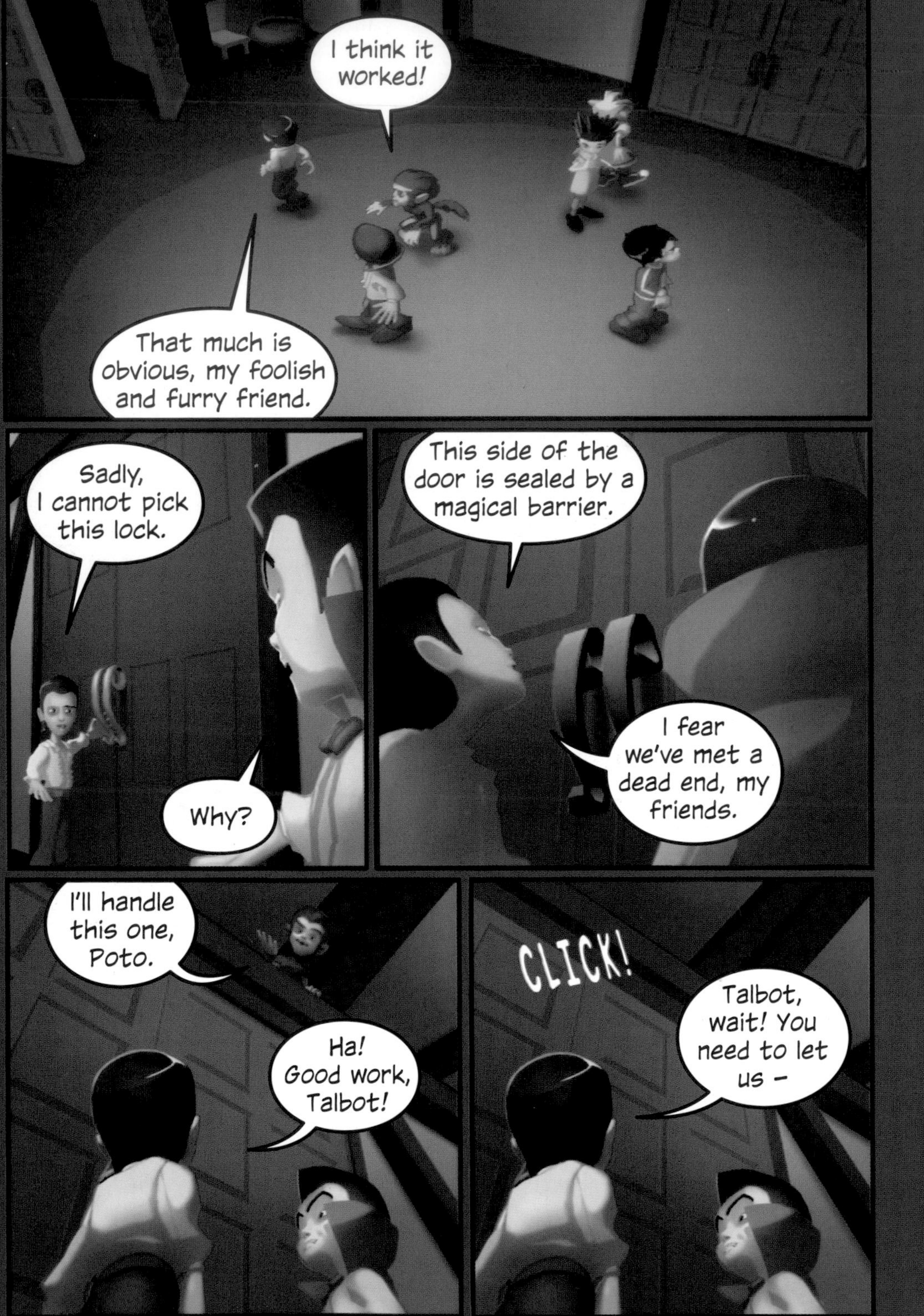
I think it worked!
That much is obvious, my foolish and furry friend.
Sadly, I cannot pick this lock.
Why?
This side of the door is sealed by a magical barrier.
I fear we've met a dead end, my friends.
I'll handle this one, Poto.
Ha! Good work, Talbot!
CLICK!
Talbot, wait! You need to let us –

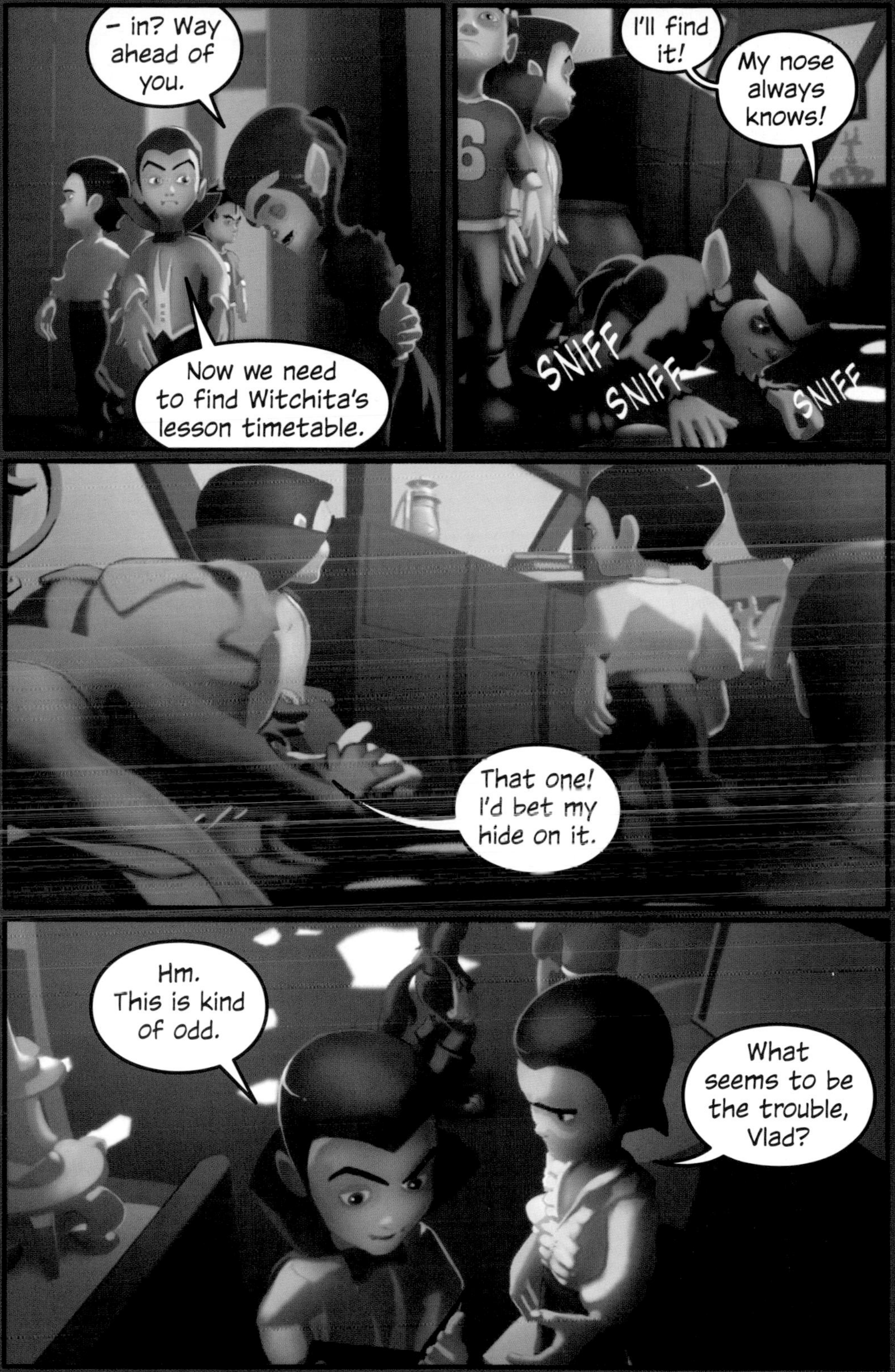
– in? Way ahead of you.
Now we need to find Witchita's lesson timetable.
I'll find it!
My nose always knows!
SNIFF
SNIFF
SNIFF
That one! I'd bet my hide on it.
Hm. This is kind of odd.
What seems to be the trouble, Vlad?

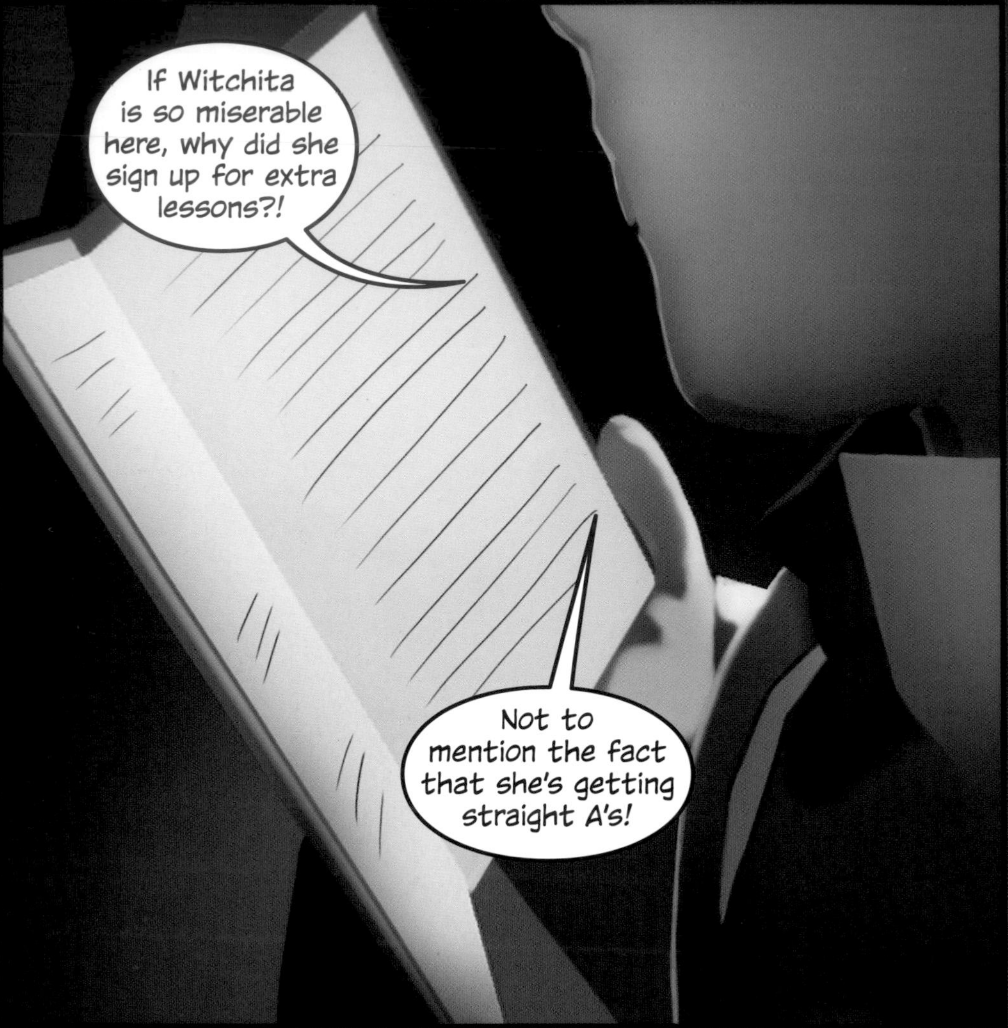
If Witchita is so miserable here, why did she sign up for extra lessons?!
Not to mention the fact that she's getting straight A's!

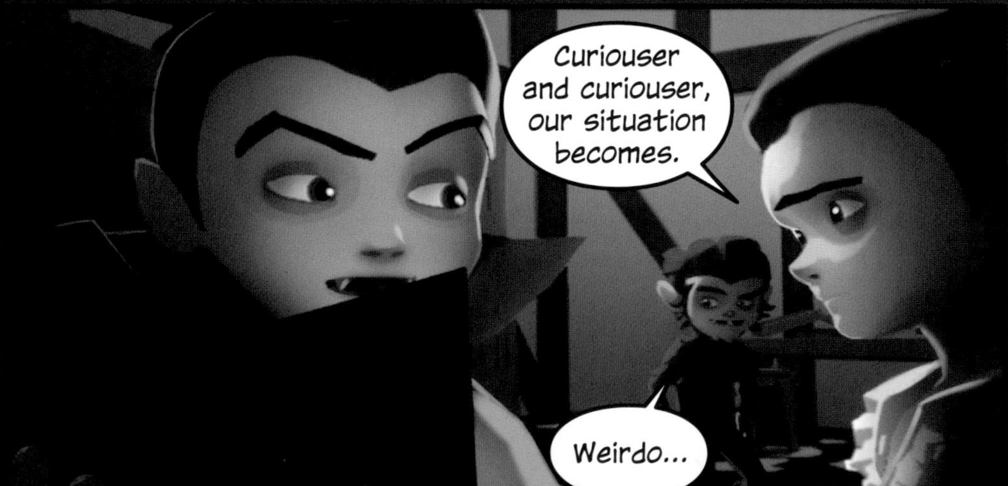
Curiouser and curiouser, our situation becomes.
Weirdo...

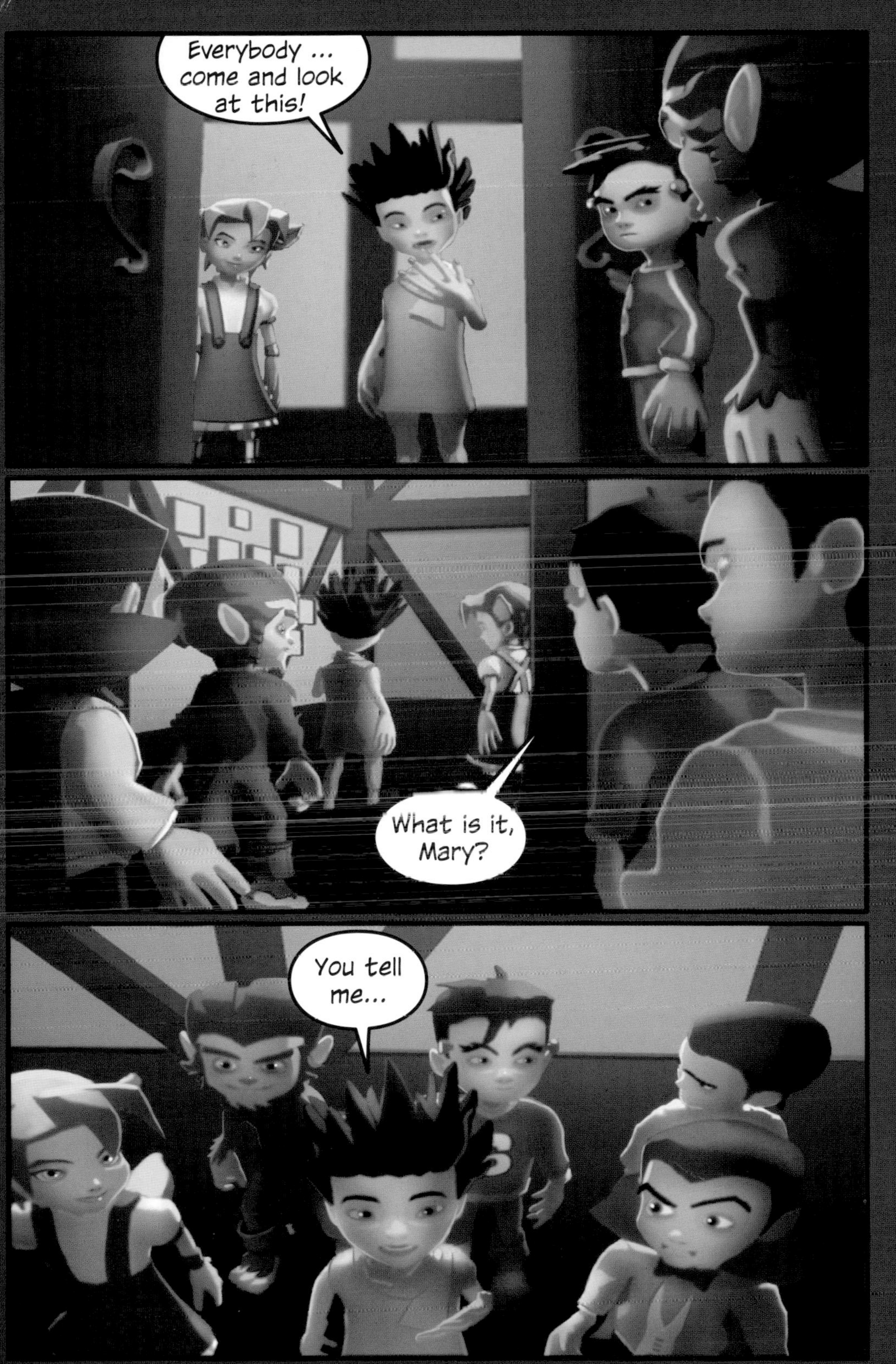
Everybody ... come and look at this!
What is it, Mary?
You tell me...

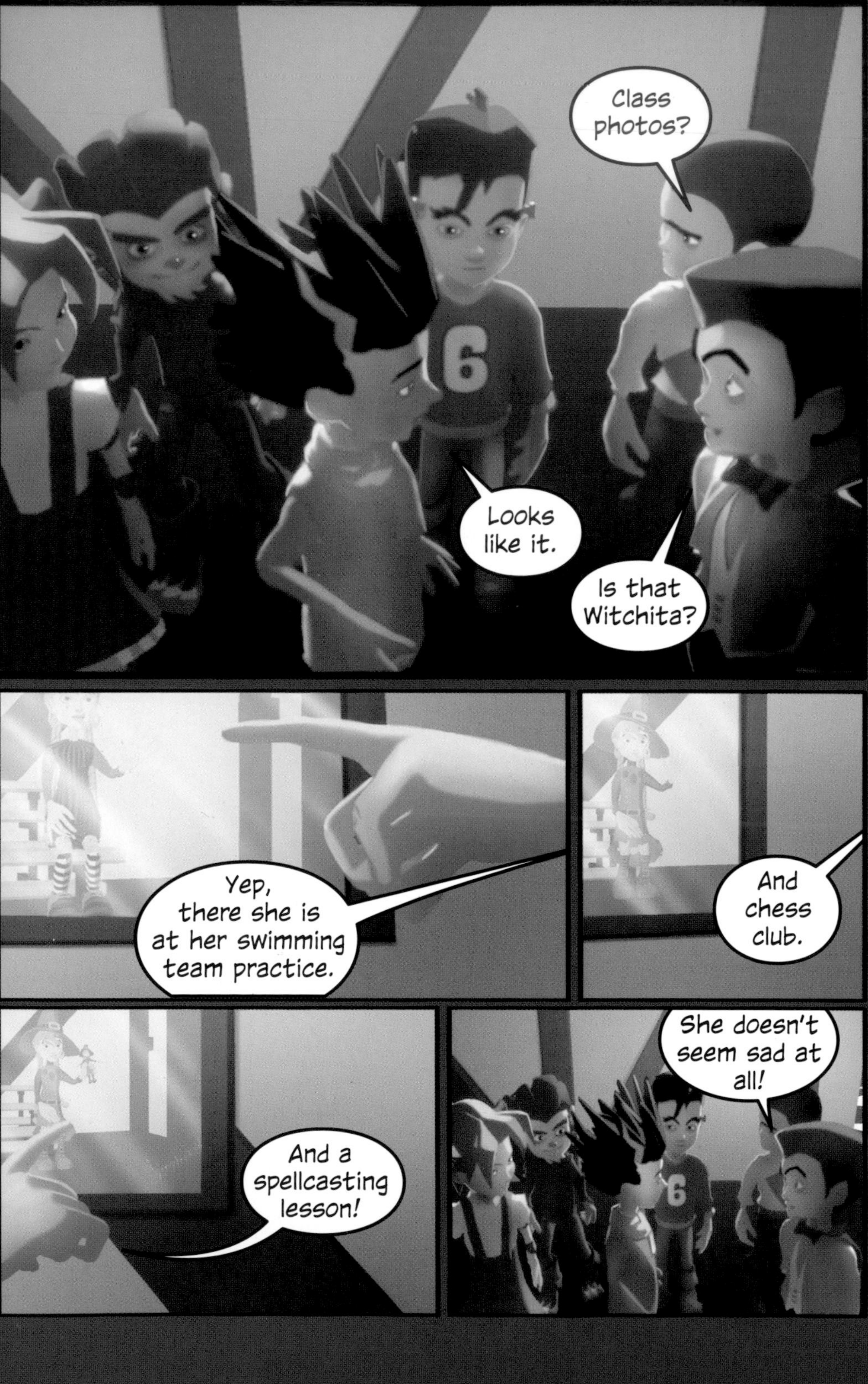
Class photos?
Looks like it.
Is that Witchita?
Yep, there she is at her swimming team practice.
And chess club.
And a spellcasting lesson!
She doesn't seem sad at all!

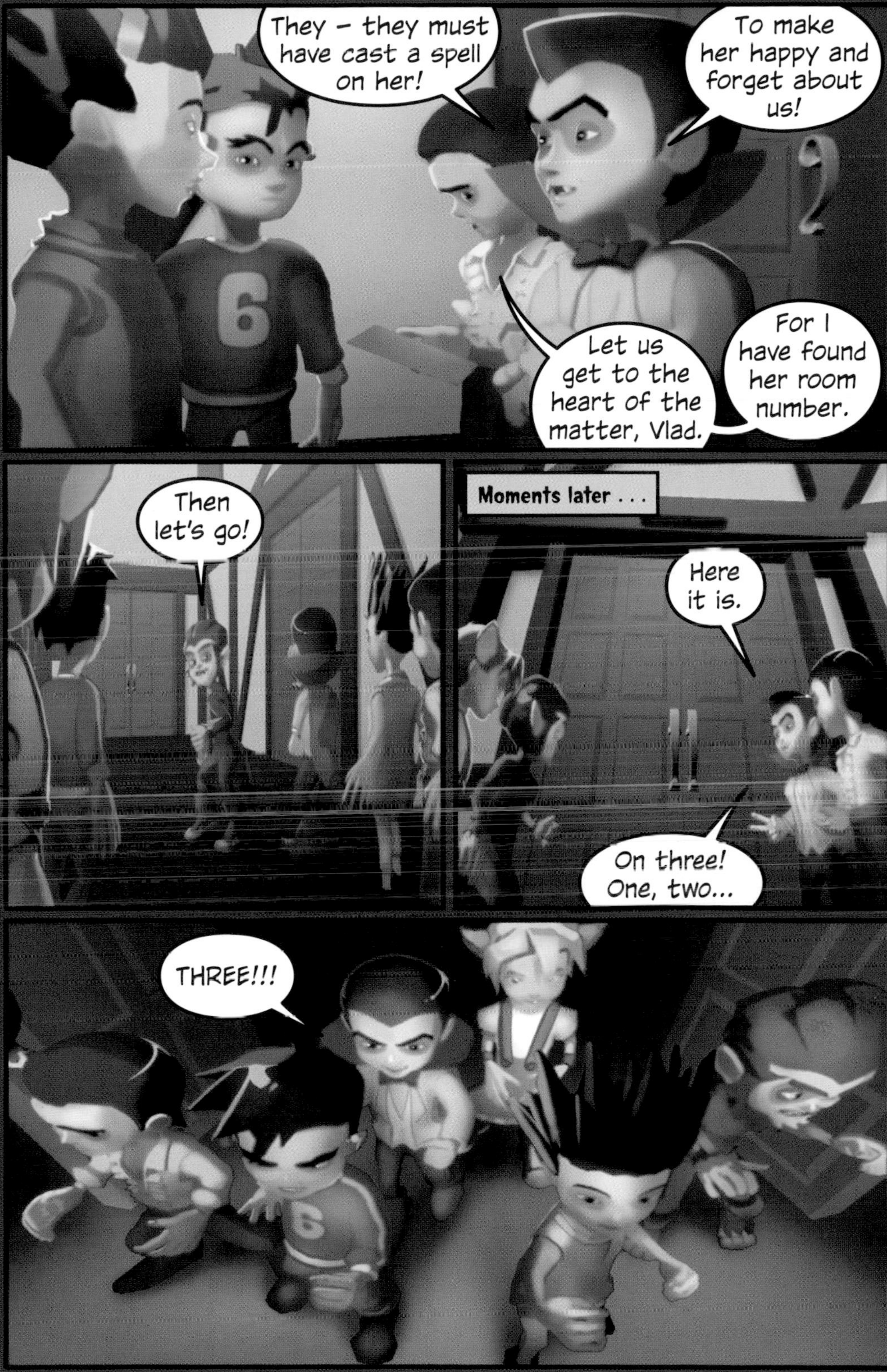
They – they must have cast a spell on her!
To make her happy and forget about us!
Let us get to the heart of the matter, Vlad.
For I have found her room number.
Then let's go!
Moments later . . .
Here it is.
On three! One, two...
THREE!!!

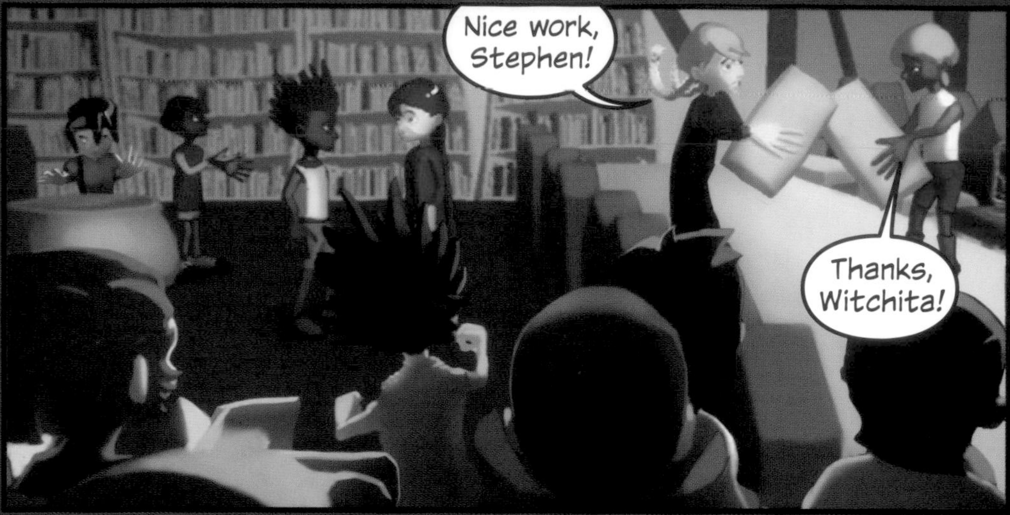
Nice work, Stephen!
Thanks, Witchita!

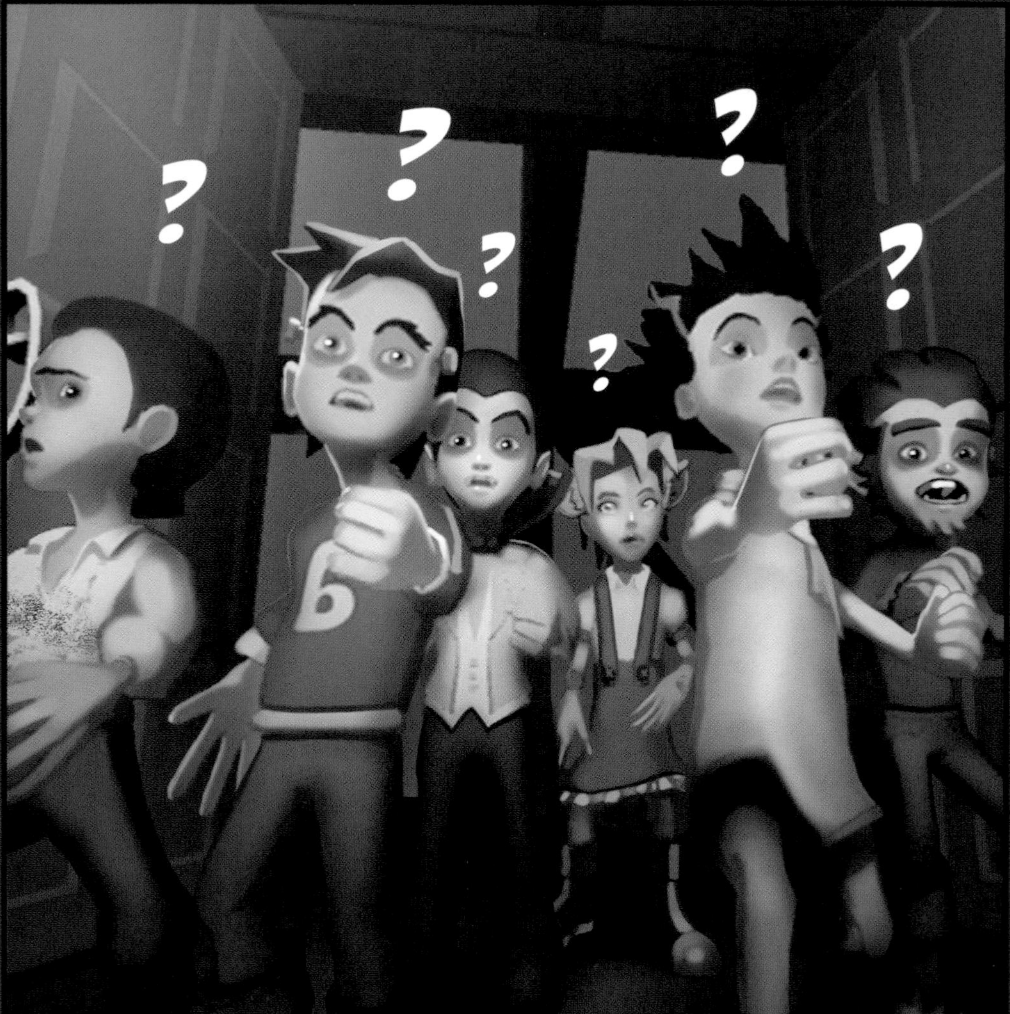
?
?
?
?
?
?

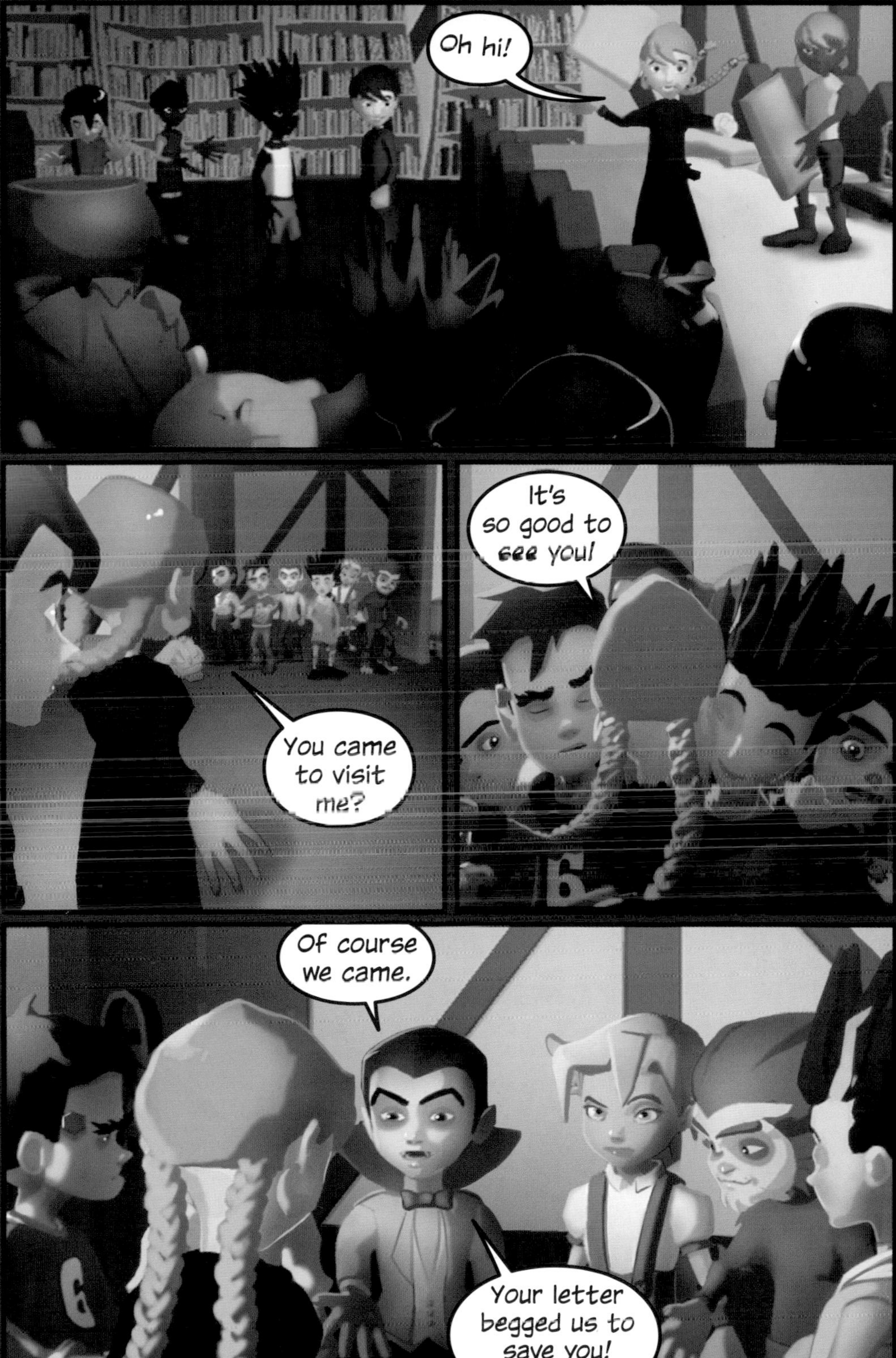
Oh hi!
You came to visit me?
It's so good to see you!
Of course we came.
Your letter begged us to save you!

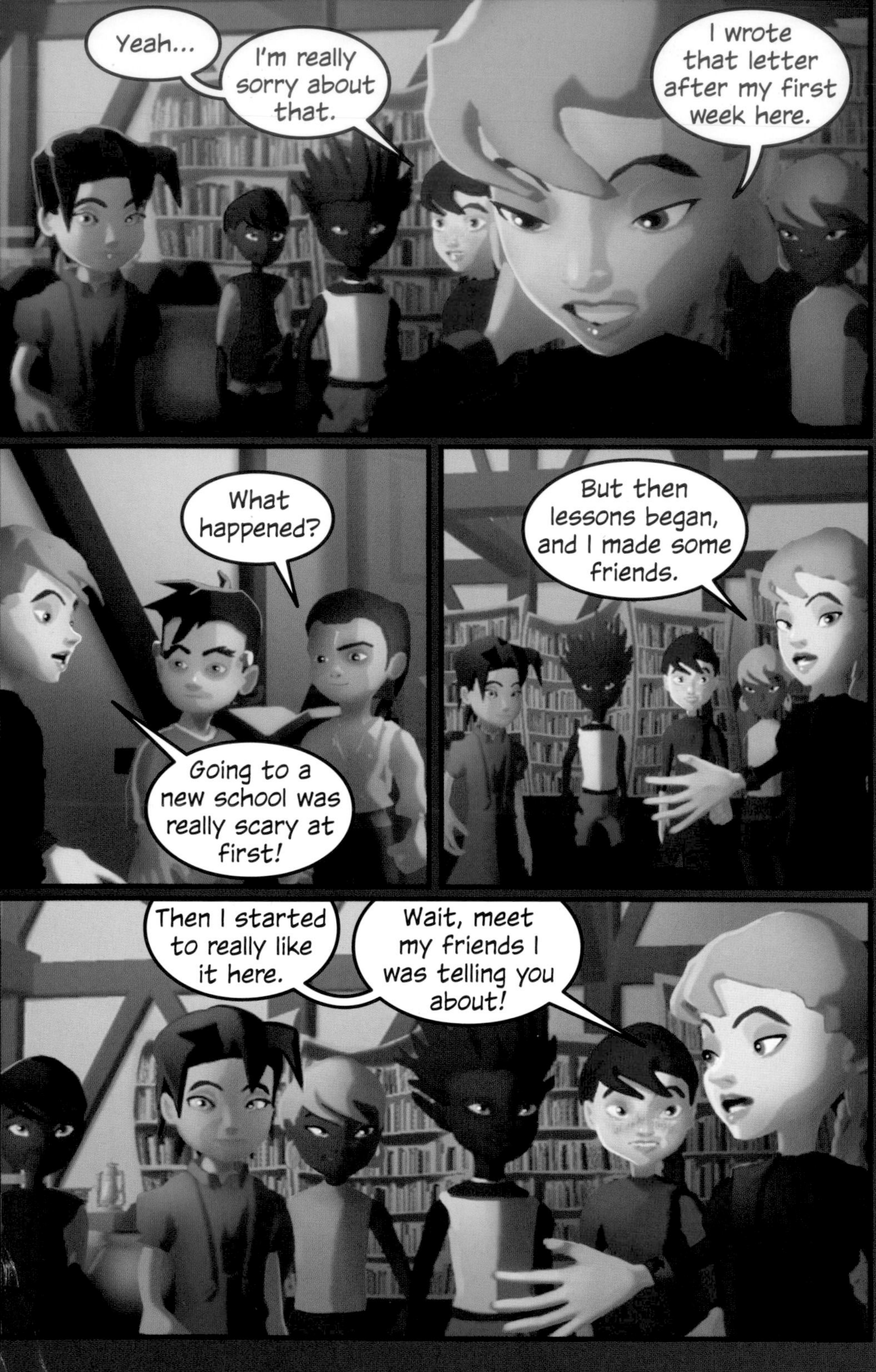
Yeah...
I'm really sorry about that.
I wrote that letter after my first week here.
What happened?
Going to a new school was really scary at first!
But then lessons began, and I made some friends.
Then I started to really like it here.
Wait, meet my friends I was telling you about!

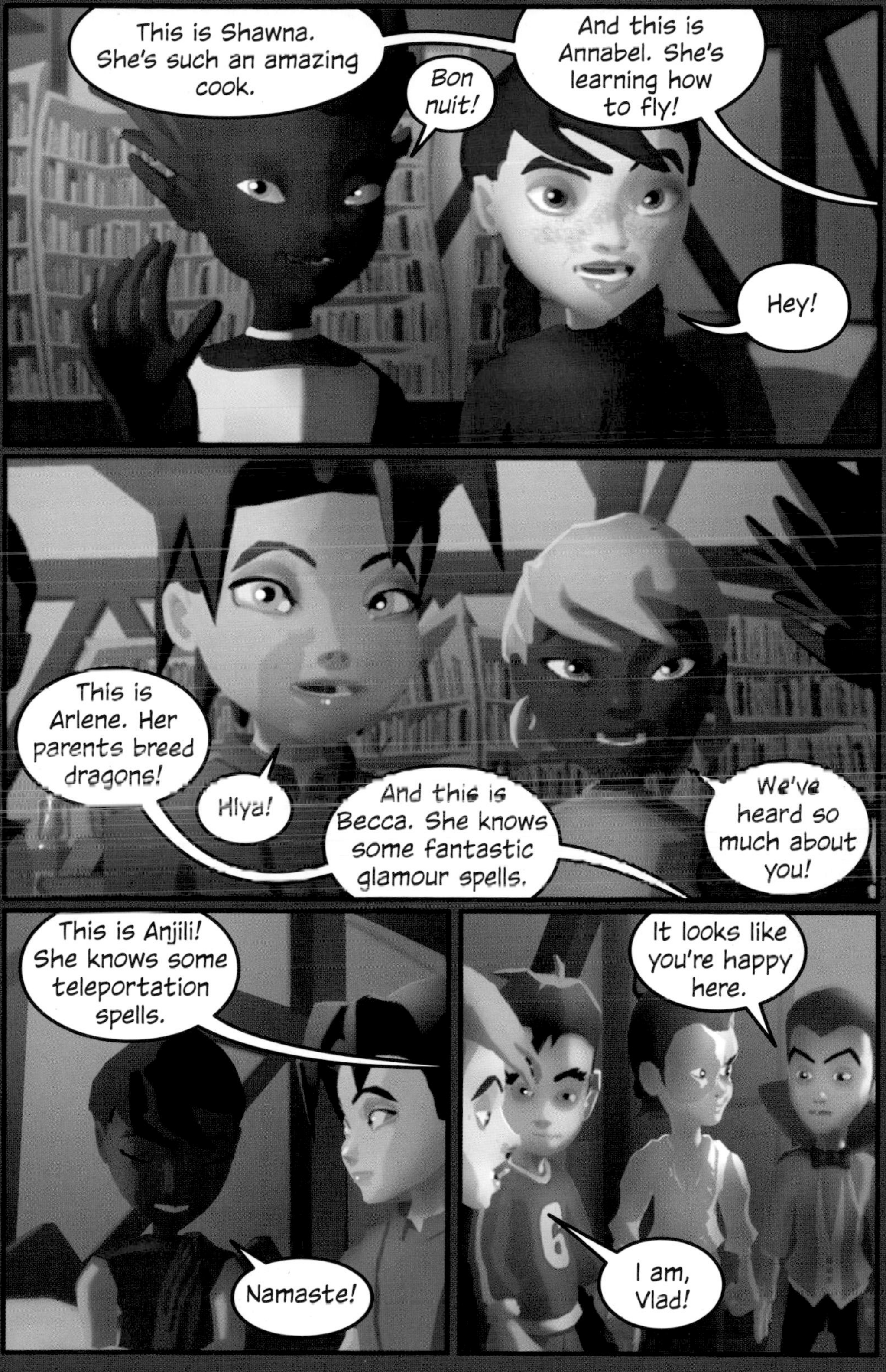
This is Shawna. She's such an amazing cook.
Bon nuit!
And this is Annabel. She's learning how to fly!
Hey!
This is Arlene. Her parents breed dragons!
Hiya!
And this is Becca. She knows some fantastic glamour spells.
We've heard so much about you!
This is Anjili! She knows some teleportation spells.
Namaste!
It looks like you're happy here.
I am, Vlad!

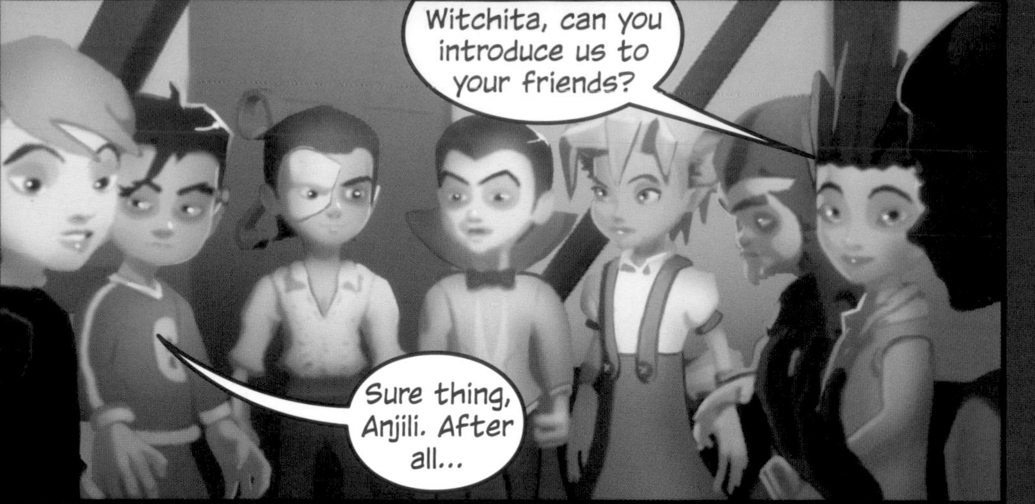
Witchita, can you introduce us to your friends?
Sure thing, Anjili. After all...

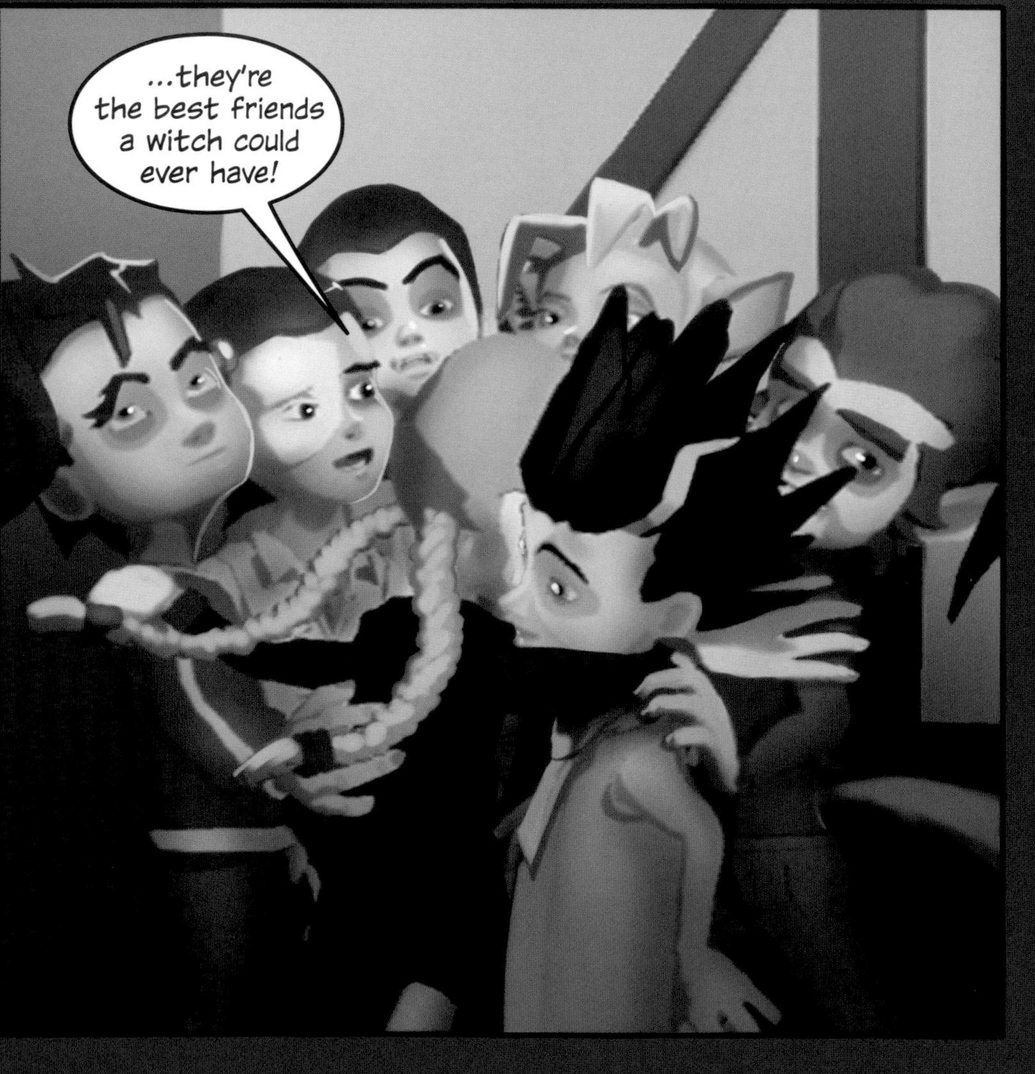
...they're the best friends a witch could ever have!

ABOUT
SEAN O'REILLY
AND ARCANA STUDIO

As a lifelong comics fan, Sean O'Reilly dreamed of becoming a comic book creator. In 2004, he realized that dream by creating Arcana Studio. In one short year, O'Reilly took his studio from a one-person operation in his basement to an award-winning comic book publisher with more than 150 graphic novels produced for Harper Collins, Simon & Schuster, Random House, Scholastic and others.

Within a year, the company won many awards including the Shuster Award for Outstanding Publisher and the Moonbeam Award for top children's graphic novel. O'Reilly also won the Top 40 Under 40 award from the city of Vancouver and authored *The Clockwork Girl* for Top Graphic Novel at Book Expo America in 2009. Currently, O'Reilly is one of the most prolific independent comic book writers in Canada. While showing no signs of slowing down in comics, he now writes screenplays and adapts his creations for the big screen.

GLOSSARY

accepted (ak-SEP-tid) – if you are accepted into something, you have been allowed to join

barrier (BA-ree-ur) – a bar, fence or wall that prevents people, traffic or other things from going past it

consequences (KON-suh-kwen-siz) – the results of an action

dire (DYE-ur) – dreadful or urgent

gifted (GIFT-id) – if you are gifted at doing something, you have a natural ability to do it

miserable (MIZ-ur-uh-buhl) – sad, unhappy or dejected

obvious (OB-vee-uhss) – easy to see or understand

rife (RIFE) – abundant, plentiful or filled with something

teleported (TEL-uh-port-id) – moved from one location to another instantly

unanimous (yoo-NAN-uh-muhss) – agreed on by everyone

DISCUSSION QUESTIONS

1. Which one of the Mighty Mighty Monsters is your favourite? Why?

2. Witchita teleports to school. Where would you go if you could teleport anywhere? Talk about travelling.

3. The gang votes to go and save Witchita from summer school. Is voting a good or bad way to solve problems? Discuss your answers.

WRITING PROMPTS

1. Imagine that you have to go to summer school. What kind of school would you go to? What would you want to learn? Write about your summer at school.

2. Each Mighty Mighty Monster has his or her own set of special skills. Imagine yourself as a monster. What kind of monster are you? What skills do you have? Write about it, then draw a picture of your monstrous self.

3. Witchita has lots of friends. How many friends do you have? Do you wish you had more? Less? What is the best amount of friends to have? Why? Write about friends.

Mighty Mighty MONSTERS ADVENTURES

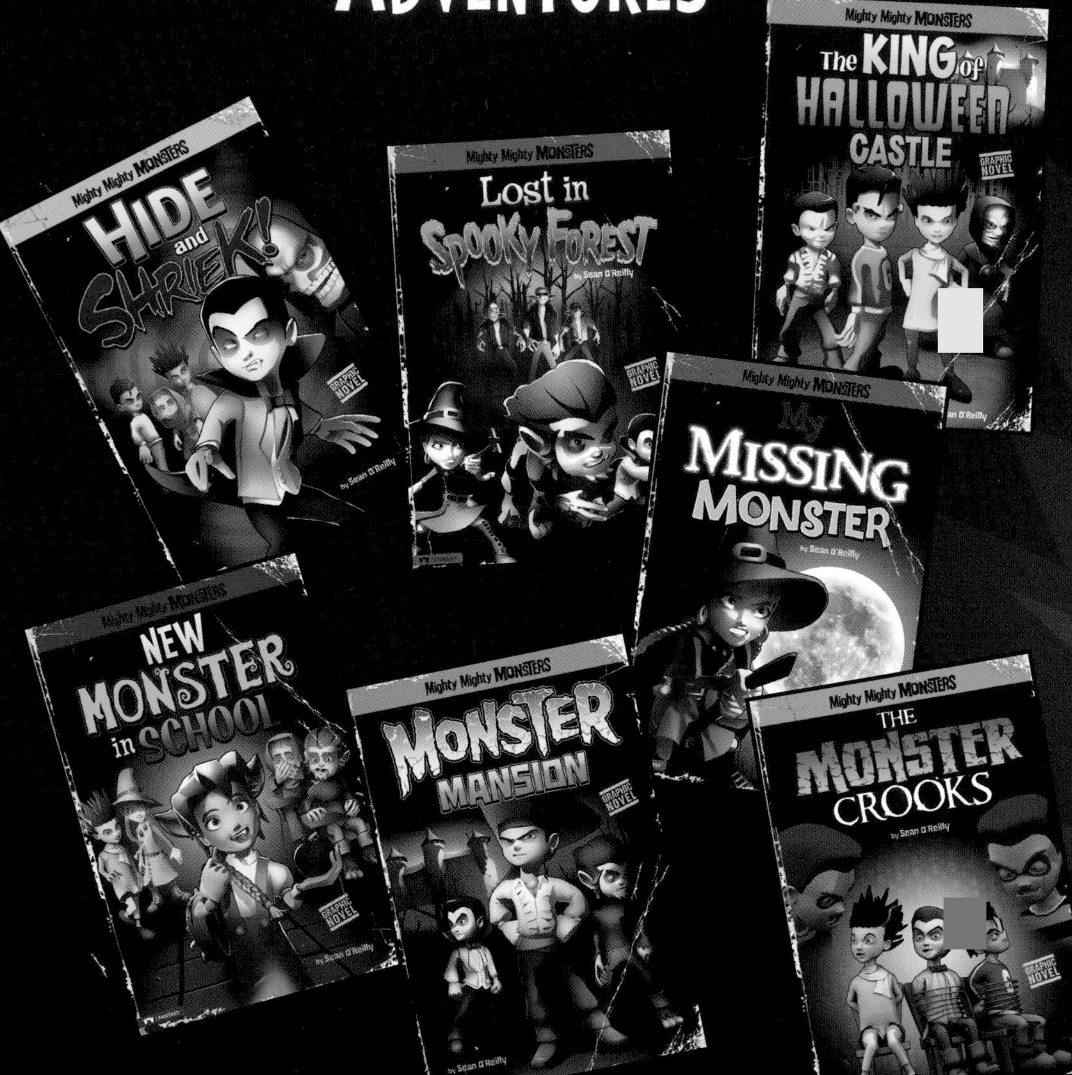
Mighty Mighty MONSTERS
The KING of HALLOWEEN CASTLE
GRAPHIC NOVEL
Mighty Mighty MONSTERS
HIDE and SHRIEK!
GRAPHIC NOVEL
by Sean O'Reilly
Mighty Mighty MONSTERS
Lost in Spooky Forest
by Sean O'Reilly
GRAPHIC NOVEL
Mighty Mighty MONSTERS
My Missing Monster
by Sean O'Reilly
Mighty Mighty MONSTERS
NEW MONSTER in SCHOOL
GRAPHIC NOVEL
by Sean O'Reilly
Mighty Mighty MONSTERS
MONSTER MANSION
GRAPHIC NOVEL
by Sean O'Reilly
Mighty Mighty MONSTERS
THE MONSTER CROOKS
by Sean O'Reilly
GRAPHIC NOVEL

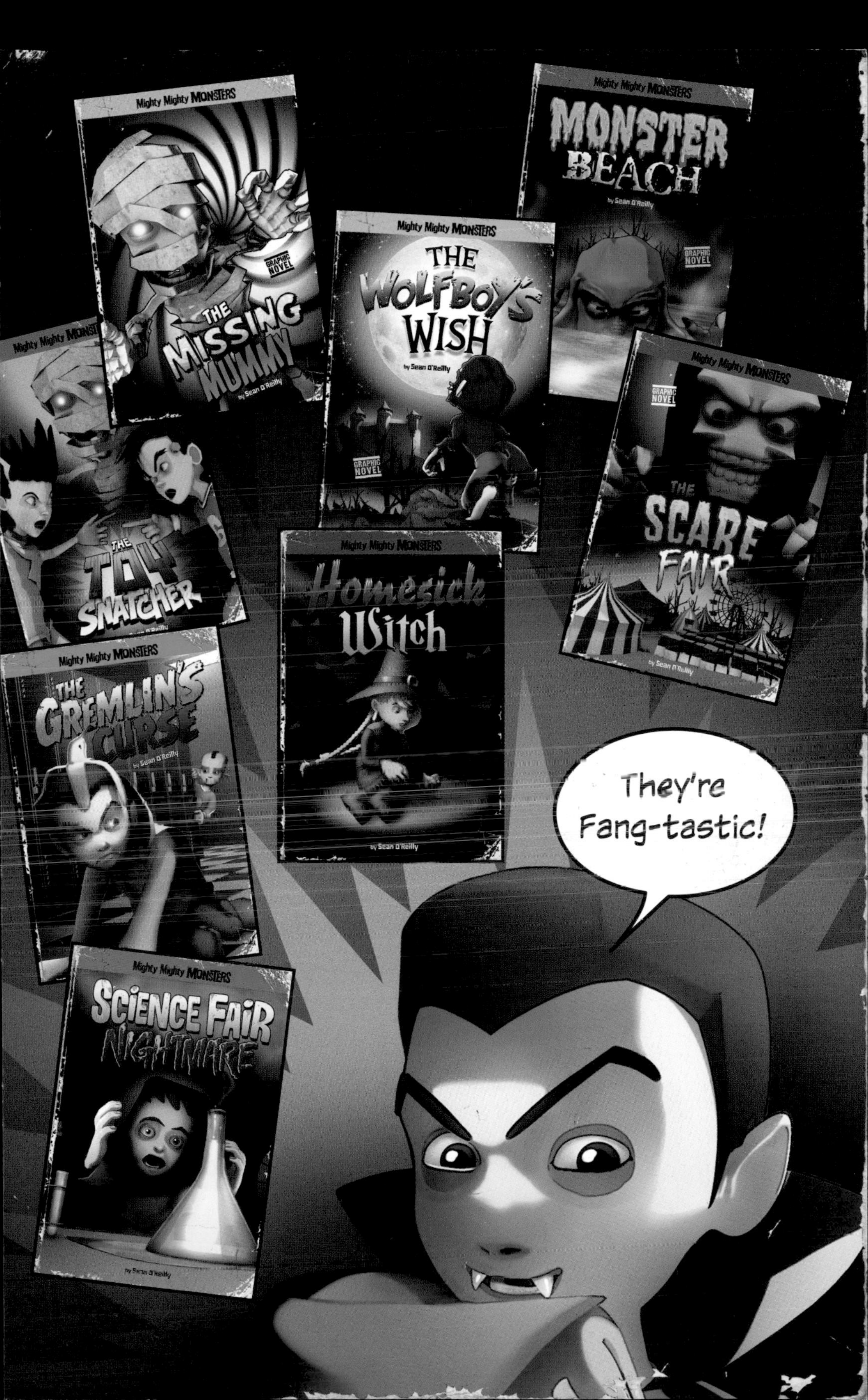
Mighty Mighty MONSTERS
THE MISSING MUMMY
by Sean O'Reilly
GRAPHIC NOVEL
Mighty Mighty MONSTERS
MONSTER BEACH
by Sean O'Reilly
GRAPHIC NOVEL
Mighty Mighty MONSTERS
THE WOLFBOY'S WISH
by Sean O'Reilly
GRAPHIC NOVEL
Mighty Mighty MONSTERS
THE TOY SNATCHER
Mighty Mighty MONSTERS
THE SCARE FAIR
GRAPHIC NOVEL
by Sean O'Reilly
Mighty Mighty MONSTERS
Homesick Witch
by Sean O'Reilly
Mighty Mighty MONSTERS
THE GREMLIN'S CURSE
by Sean O'Reilly
Mighty Mighty MONSTERS
SCIENCE FAIR NIGHTMARE
by Sean O'Reilly
They're Fang-tastic!

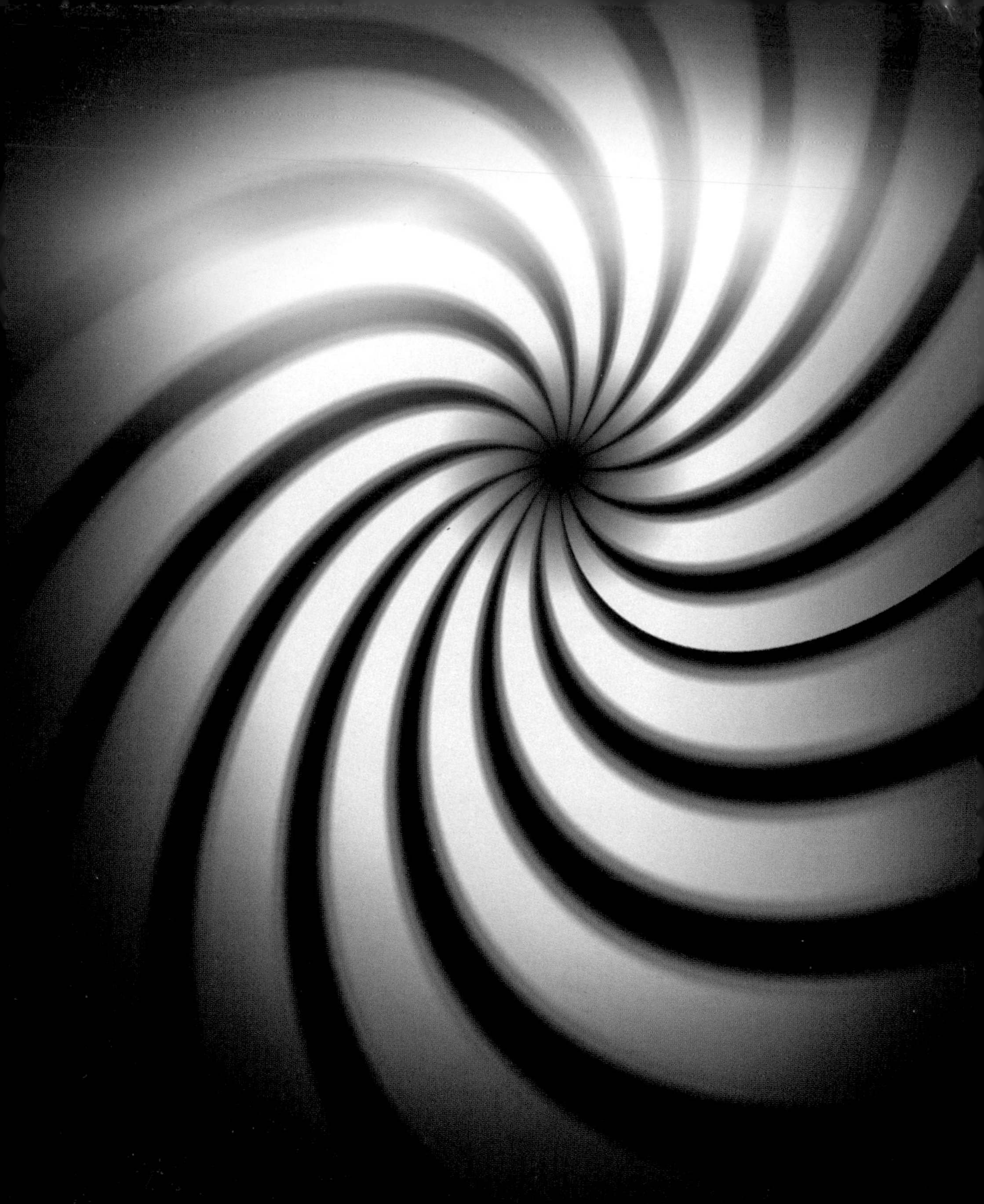

www.raintree.co.uk